A LOOK
INTO
THE HUMAN HEART

in a panoply of tales that will entertain, absorb, disturb—and inspire—readers of all tastes, all backgrounds.

Jesus, the master storyteller, knew that men understand truth most easily when their imagination is stirred, and brought His Word to the people in parables.

Writers and storytellers from tribe to metropolis have known that basic wisdom as well.

And in **How Silently, How Silently**, the reader may look and see what Joseph Bayly is saying as he opens the doors to imagination and perception in an extraordinary collection of parables for our times.

BOOKS BY JOSEPH BAYLY

THE GOSPEL BLIMP

MARTYRED

THE VIEW FROM A HEARSE

OUT OF MY MIND

WHAT ABOUT HOROSCOPES?

PSALMS OF MY LIFE

HOW SILENTLY, HOW SILENTLY

How Silently, How Silently

and
Other Stories

by Joseph Bayly

David C. Cook Publishing Co.
850 NORTH GROVE AVENUE • ELGIN, IL 60120
In Canada: David C. Cook Publishing (Canada) Ltd., Weston, Ontario M9L 1T4

HOW SILENTLY, HOW SILENTLY

Formerly published as I SAW GOOLEY FLY
Library of Congress Catalog Number: 68-28433

David C. Cook Publishing Co., Elgin, IL 60120

Printed in the United States of America
Library of Congress Catalog Number: 73-86827
ISBN: O-912692-24-3

FOR MARY LOU

as a grace note
to thirty years

Contents

How Silently, How Silently

HE ARRIVED at Chicago's O'Hare airport on TWA flight 801 from Israel. The plane was two hours late, but the delay made little difference, since there was no one to meet him.

It was December twenty-third, a Friday afternoon. The terminal building pulsed with people coming home for Christmas, relatives meeting people coming home, businessmen and students trying to get on flights for Cleveland and New York, Seattle and Atlanta, so they could be home for the holidays.

The Israeli had gone through immigration and customs in New York. He had no baggage, only a small airline bag with a broken zipper.

Christmas carols issued from concealed speakers the length of a long corridor into the main building, interrupted only by announcements of arriving flights, departing flights, boarding areas now open, passengers being paged.

9

He walked down the corridor listening, watching people.

In the main terminal building a massive, white-flocked Christmas tree, decorated with golden balls, stood in a corner beyond the telephone booths and rows of seats. He turned aside to examine the tree, then stepped onto an escalator marked "Down to Baggage and Ground Transportation."

"Excuse me," he said to a pretty girl at the Avis counter, "can you tell me how to get to Wheaton, Illinois?"

"Easiest way is to rent an Avis car and drive there," she replied. "Only thing, we don't have any available. I'm sorry. Unless you have a reservation, that is. If you don't, you might try Number One over there."

"Thank you, but I don't drive. Is there a bus?"

"I don't think so. You'll have to take a cab."

He repeated his question to a man in uniform who stood near the door of the terminal, explaining that he didn't think he had enough money for a cab.

"Take this bus to the Loop," the man said. "Get off at the Palmer House, walk back to State Street, down State to Madison—get that? On Madison get a bus to North Western Station. You can get a train there for Wheaton. Bus is loading now."

The young Israeli murmured his thanks and walked outside the terminal building. He shivered as the sharp wind whipped through his light topcoat. It was snowing.

"Please tell me when we get to the Palmer House," he asked the bus driver.

"First stop," the driver said.

The bus cruised down the expressway. Lights and signs and thousands of cars. Trucks and shopping centers and Christmas trees and lights. Signboards in green and red, "Merry Christmas" in letters two feet high.

"Palmer House," the driver called.

The Israeli left the warm bus. A blast of cold air off the

lake hit him as he stepped down to the sidewalk. His teeth chattered; he turned the ineffectual collar of his coat up around his neck.

At the corner he hesitated, then stopped to look at the jewels and expensive ornaments in Peacock's window. Then he hurried on, after asking a policeman which direction Madison Street was.

Almost running because of the cold wind and driving snow, he covered the three blocks to the other bus quickly. It was crowded; he stood between an elderly woman who kept sneezing into the elbow of her ragged coat, and a teenage boy, his arms full of packages.

At the North Western Station he bought a ticket to Wheaton, then sat in the waiting room for half an hour. Once he went over to the newsstand to buy a paper. The front page had stories about war, politics, crime; a photograph of a wan child with leukemia, slumped in a wheelchair beside a smiling actress and a Christmas tree at Children's Hospital; a reminder of "One Shopping Day Left Before Christmas."

Finally he boarded the train. It was so hot inside, and he was so tired from his trip, which had started the previous day in the Middle East, that he fell asleep.

About an hour later the conductor shook him awake. "You want to get off at Wheaton, this is it."

The young Israeli stepped down onto the snow-covered station platform. He almost fell as his foot slipped on the smooth surface.

"Careful there, young fellow." The conductor clutched his arm.

He crossed the tracks to the sidewalk. As he looked uncertainly in both directions, a young woman smiled at him. She was leaning against a green Vega.

"Hi," she called.

"Hello," he answered. "So this is Wheaton."

"It is, for better or for worse."

"Is there any worse?"

"Yes. Me, for instance. You look cold—where you going?"

"I'm not sure."

"It's darned cold talking out here. How about coming up to my apartment? It's only a few blocks over—I'll drive you."

"Thank you. Do you live with your mother or someone?"

"No, I live alone. Say, are you from around here? Or maybe Glen Ellyn? I saw you get off the train."

"I'm from Israel."

"You're Jewish, aren't you?"

"Yes, I'm Jewish. And you're Mary."

"How did you know? Did someone tell you about me?" An edge of belligerence showed in her voice.

"You had to be Mary."

"What do you mean, I had to be Mary? Why couldn't I be Judy, or Jean, or Connie?"

"Because you're Mary."

"If you're from Israel, you're a long way from home. Do you have any friends here? I mean, is anyone expecting you?"

"Nobody's expecting me. And I haven't a place to stay, so I'm in the market for one."

"You can stay with me for a few days."

"Thank you, Mary. Any other suggestions?"

"I mean it. It'll be nice having company over Christmas. You won't put me out."

"Mary, I do appreciate your invitation, I do. But are there any other possibilities?"

"Well, there's a house over near my apartment building, where the lady takes roomers. She's really old—and safe. Maybe she'd have a room for you."

"Would you drive me there so I can find out?"

"Sure. Get in the car—you must be freezing."

12

"I am. This coat was made for Jerusalem, not Chicago."

"Or Wheaton. This is a cold place, too."

The elderly lady had a room, which the Israeli took. He had barely enough money for one week's rent.

Mary saw him count out the bills, and saw how little was left in his wallet.

"Look," she said, "I just got paid. Let me give you something to tide you over."

"Mary, you're generous. I don't think I'll need it, though. After all, I'll only be here over Christmas."

"Well, as long as you don't forget that I'm ready to help you—no strings attached."

"No strings attached."

"Hey, it's almost seven o'clock and I haven't eaten yet."

"We had a big meal on the plane from New York, so I'm not hungry."

"Good. In that case I know where we can get enough to eat without having to pay for it. This Christian publishing company is having a sort of Christmas open house this evening. The public's invited to see their new building. We can go and fill up on cookies and punch."

"Sounds interesting. Let's go."

Mary drove several miles, then parked her car in the parking lot of a rather imposing one-story building.

"Look here," she said as they closed the car doors, "we don't have to stay very long."

"All right, Mary. By the way, what are those other buildings?"

"That one's Christian Youth headquarters, the next one's Sunday School, the one down the road there is Congo Missions. Let's get in out of the cold."

Inside the building, a table was placed in front of a Christmas tree. The tree was decorated with hundreds of little Bibles, about the size of a child's hand, hanging from the branches.

The table was covered with a white cloth and decorated

with holly. A poinsettia plant in the center was surrounded by sandwiches, Christmas cookies, a silver coffee service, plates, cups, napkins and spoons. An empty punchbowl stood at one end of the table.

"I'm sorry we've run out of punch," said the lady seated at the other end of the table. "May I pour you some coffee?"

"Yes, please." Mary extended her hand for the cup.

"Could you get me some water, please?" asked the young Israeli. "Maybe just fill up the punchbowl."

"Oh, we won't need to do that," the lady replied. "That many people won't be wanting water tonight."

"Why don't you do like he says?" Mary asked. "Maybe he's really thirsty. Or maybe some other people will be. It's hot in here, you know. Or hadn't you noticed?"

"Certainly," the lady said. "Bob, could you come here a moment? Will you please fill the punchbowl up with water? Thanks."

Bob returned after several minutes, carrying the large bowl awkwardly because of its weight.

"Strangest thing happened," he said in an excited voice. "When I took it out in the kitchen it was empty, except for some ice. But when I turned the faucet on, and began filling the bowl, it wasn't like water at all. Look, it's dark red."

"Let's have a taste."

"I can't believe it, I really can't. There's—yes, I'm sure it's wine in that punchbowl. Bob, tell us the truth. What really happened?"

"Just like I said. When the water from the kitchen faucet ran into the punchbowl, it turned to what's in there now. Honest it did."

"I haven't tasted that stuff in fifteen years, not since I was saved. But there's no doubt about it—that's wine, and it's the best."

"Bob, will you please take it back out in the kitchen

and pour it down the drain? We can't have word get around that we served an alcoholic beverage here at our open house.

"I'm sorry about what's happened, sir," she said to the Israeli. "Would you like some coffee?"

"No, thank you. I'll just have some of these sandwiches and cookies."

A few minutes later, Mary suggested they leave. And they did.

"That was great," she said as they drove away in her car. "I don't know how you did it, but it was just great."

"I'm tired—I guess it must be the time change from Israel to here. You won't mind driving me back to my room now?"

"Of course not. And I won't even try to get you to stop at my apartment first."

Next morning the young Israeli slept late. When he left the house, he saw Mary waiting in her car at the corner. It had snowed all night, and the heavy flakes were still coming down.

"How long have you been waiting here?" he asked, as he opened the car door.

"Oh, ten—maybe fifteen minutes. That's all."

"It would have taken a lot longer than that for the windshield to get this covered with snow." As he sat down in the warm car, he brushed the snow from his thin topcoat.

"Hey, I have something for you," she said.

"What is it, Mary? Say, will you please turn that radio down? I can hardly hear you, and I feel as if I have to shout to make myself heard."

"Sure. That's WLS, by the way. Here's what I got for you."

"A heavy coat and earmuffs! Mary, Mary. You knew how cold I was, and you bought me some warm clothes. Do you mind if I put them on right now?"

15

"I'll mind if you don't."

As they sat at breakfast in a small restaurant, Mary and the Israeli were silent for a long time. Finally the Israeli spoke.

"Mary, you're sick of it, aren't you?"

"Up to here." She put her hand to her mouth.

"Things will be different."

"They already are. I know you now. Please stay for a while."

"Not for long."

"Long enough to make sure the change is permanent?"

"It will be. I don't need to stay around here for that, Mary."

"Long enough to change this town?"

"No, I can't stay that long. Just until tomorrow night."

"Christmas night."

"Christmas night. Then I must leave."

"It's funny, having you here in Wheaton for Christmas. And funnier that I'm the only one who knows you're here."

"You were there at the North Western Station to meet me."

"Am I glad I was!"

"Let's finish our coffee and leave."

"Look, I have to work this afternoon. You take my car—you can drop me off, and maybe pick me up around six o'clock. Or I can walk home. It's not far. But you can use my car to get around in today."

"I don't drive. Thanks anyway, Mary. But I'll manage without transportation today. Especially with this warm coat." He smiled at her.

"Do you like it? I hoped you would. Now I'll have to get to work. How about meeting me for supper tonight? I'll stop by your house for you at six-thirty or seven. Then later we can go to the Christmas Eve service at church. I haven't been there for a while, but I'd like to go again.

"Fine, Mary. I'll be looking for you around six-thirty."

He walked all over town that afternoon, stopping at the county jail, a convalescent home, and the church parsonage.

A middle-aged, worried-looking woman answered the door at the parsonage.

"Yes?" she said.

"I am a stranger here, from Israel. I thought I'd stop by to meet the pastor."

"He's very busy today—the day before Christmas, you know, and Christmas on a Sunday this year. But step inside, I'll call him."

He waited inside the door for several minutes. Then the pastor came downstairs with his wife.

"James, this is a man from Israel who wants to meet you. I told him how busy you are this afternoon."

"Never too busy to meet one of the Lord's people. Welcome!" He gripped the younger man's hand. "Are you here for long?"

"Just through Christmas. I'll probably leave tomorrow night."

"Well, it's great to meet you. Will you be in church tomorrow? We're especially interested in Israel—our church supports two missionaries there. Israel General Mission. Know it?"

"I've heard of it."

" 'To the Jew first,' I always say. Maybe you'd share something with us at our morning service tomorrow. Our missionary conference is coming up in February and it won't hurt a bit to have a word about Israel and missions on Christmas Sunday morning."

"I'll be glad to speak."

"Just briefly, you understand. Five minutes at the most. We'll really be pushed for time tomorrow—special music, you know. Probably you have the same problem with time back home in Israel."

17

"Perhaps things are a little more simple there. Yes, I'll stick to the five minutes."

"Good. The Lord bless you. Is it still snowing out? I'll see you tomorrow—don't trip on the raised sill."

The Israeli returned to his room in the house where he was staying.

A little after six-thirty he saw the green Vega parked in front of the house. He heard a light sound of the horn as he went downstairs, pulling on his new warm coat.

Mary leaned over to open the door. "It's great to see you again. I thought the afternoon would never end."

"I guess my afternoon went quickly because I did so much walking and saw so many different people. But I'm certainly glad to see you again, Mary."

"Look, is it all right with you if we go up to my apartment to eat?" Before he could answer, she added, "There will be other people there, friends of mine."

"I'd like nothing better."

"But we'll probably get talking and won't get to the Christmas Eve service at church. In fact, these friends of mine wouldn't go anyway. They're not the church kind. They're like me—like I was before I met you."

"Supper with you and your friends sounds a lot more interesting—and worthwhile—than sitting through a Christmas Eve service."

"Do you really mean it? I was afraid you'd be like the rest—oh, that wasn't a kind thing to say. I've got so much to learn."

By now they were climbing the stairs to the second-floor apartment. From inside the door came sounds of the Living Dead.

"It'll be noisy," Mary said as she opened the door. "Hi," she called out to the six or seven forms sprawled on chairs and on the floor. "Turn that record player down, someone. I want you all to meet my new friend. I've only known him one day, but in my whole life nobody has ever known me so well. He's from Israel."

"Welcome, Israeli. How are the Arabs?"

"Suffering, as they have for centuries. Like my own people."

"We'll eat soon, gang," Mary called as she went into the tiny kitchen. She turned toward the Israeli: "Come and help me."

Before long, spaghetti was overflowing a large bowl, and long loaves of bread, buttered and flavored with garlic, were placed on the table next to a bowl of green salad. The table had no cloth on it. Paper plates and red paper napkins were set out, with stainless steel utensils.

When the food was on the table, Mary announced, "Before we eat, my Israeli friend will pray."

There was a whisper, "Mary has a new hangup."

The Israeli stood in the kitchen doorway. "Father," he said, "I thank you for this spaghetti and for Mary's kindness to us all. Make your name glorious in this room tonight."

No one sat at the table. They ate from their laps, or placed their plates on the floor, where they sat or reclined. At first the music was so loud it was hard to talk, except to one other person. But as they were finishing the meal, Mary turned down the volume. Then the whole group began to discuss war and peace, sex and drugs, life, race (two of them were black), Camus and Christmas.

The Israeli listened most of the time, although he asked a lot of questions. His occasional comments were brief. He also told several stories.

As the evening passed, they began to ask him questions. His answers were direct, without pressure.

At midnight Mary said, "Merry Christmas, Israeli! Merry Christmas, everyone!"

Soon afterward the guests began to leave. The Israeli was the last to go.

"Thanks for a most enjoyable Christmas Eve, Mary.

19

And thank you for introducing me to your friends. They're an interesting group, each one different."

"Thank you for coming. May I go to church with you tomorrow?"

"Of course. I was hoping you would."

"I'll stop at your house about ten-thirty."

"Fine. Good night, Mary."

He walked through the snow—by now almost to his knees—to the house where he was staying. Because most of the sidewalks were not yet shoveled, he walked in the street, where cars had smoothed some narrow tracks.

In his room he undressed, then stood by the window for a moment, shivering in the darkness, looking at the silent snow. He prayed, "Father, I thank you that you hear me. I thank you that things shall not always be as they were that night and as they are this night. Cover earth with righteousness and justice and love as snow covers all things tonight."

He slept.

The blinding sunlight of Christmas morning awoke him, reflecting whiteness all around. From his airline bag he removed an orange, which he peeled and ate.

Just before ten-thirty, Mary came. The green Vega was filled with the people who had been at her apartment the previous evening—all except one couple, who rode a motorcycle behind Mary's car. A snowplow had partially cleared the street.

"Merry Christmas, Israeli!" they all shouted as he came out of the house.

He smiled—a pleased, happy smile. "Thank you, friends. And Merry Christmas to all of you. I'm surprised to see you, but I'm glad you're going to the service with Mary and me."

"Mary didn't twist our arms, either," one said. "Yesterday she'd have had to, and we still wouldn't have gone. The fact is, she wouldn't have gone herself, before yesterday. But now we've met you ourselves, and we know you, so we want to go."

At the church, which was already almost full, an usher led them up to a partially empty pew at the very front. They were an odd assortment: mini-skirted, leather-coated, long haired, one bearded, two black skinned and the rest white. And the Israeli, who sat between Mary and a young black man.

The service began with the doxology and Apostles' Creed. Carols sung by the congregation, "O Holy Night" by the combined choirs, the Christmas story from Luke's Gospel followed. Next the offering. While the ushers were taking it, and the organ was playing, the pastor looked thoughtfully down at the front pew, at the Israeli and the group of young men and women around him.

After the offering, the children's choir sang "Silent Night."

The sermon followed. It was a carefully prepared, almost exhaustive survey of the Old Testament prophetic passages that predicted Christ's advent.

A prayer, "O Little Town of Bethlehem," and the benediction ended the service.

Mary's little group of friends surrounded the Israeli as they walked behind the slow-moving group out the center aisle. The young black man turned to him. "Sir, could I talk to you before you leave town? Mary says you're heading back out today."

"Of course. We'll find a quiet place."

At the door, the pastor smiled as he shook their hands. "I hope you all felt welcome among us. And you, my friend," taking the Israeli's hand, "I'm sorry there just wasn't time in the service for a word from you. But Christmas morning, you know—people are so anxious for the service to end promptly at twelve so they can get home to their family celebrations and opening the presents. I hope you understand."

"I do," said the Israeli.

Mary spoke to the pastor. "You missed something. We know, because we've been listening to him."

"Well, Merry Christmas," said the pastor, turning from them to greet the last ones to leave.

They went back to Mary's apartment for a bacon-and-eggs lunch. They talked all afternoon.

Around five o'clock Mary drove the Israeli to O'Hare airport. Everybody went. This time the motorcycle, with its two riders, led the way.

He left for Israel on TWA Flight 802.

I Saw Gooley Fly

HERB GOOLEY was just an ordinary sort of guy until the night he stepped out of his third-floor dorm window and flew away into the wild blue yonder.

But I'm getting ahead of my story.

I first met Gooley in that little hamburger and malt joint just off campus—Pete's Place. I'd never have noticed the guy except that he dropped a mustard bottle, and the stuff squirted down the front of his storm jacket. Now I'm a sophomore at the time and this guy's a frosh. (No mistaking them during those early weeks of the quarter.) But he's making such a mess out of wiping the stuff off that I help him. Brother, what a mess. But Herb was the sort of fellow who could hardly wipe his nose himself, let alone the mustard.

When we had the stuff pretty well wiped off his coat and shirt (you could still see these bright yellow streaks), I ask him where he sacks out.

23

"Pollard," he says.

"That hole. Must be a frosh, huh? You'll learn. 'Course you can transfer after a quarter. Me, I'm at Sigma Phi House. Know the place that looks like a country club over on Lincoln?"

He doesn't know it. So we pay Pete and walk out. That is, I walk out. Herb trips over a cigarette machine that stands near the door.

Next time I notice the guy is at Homecoming.

It's during the frosh-soph tug-of-war. (They really had pressure on those fire hoses that year.) We're ready for the final pull and the gun goes off. Suddenly the whole frosh team's yelling to stop pulling. So, after they turn the hoses on us, we stop; and here's Gooley, looking sort of dazed, with the rope twisted clear around his arm. I'll never know how he did it. They get it off and take him to the infirmary. Nothing broken, but he sure must have had a painful arm for a few days.

I remember—sometime the following fall—seeing a crowd gathered around the front of Hinton's department store. So I pull over to the curb, and here is the college station wagon half-in, half-out of Hinton's show window. What a scene. Bodies all over the place, one of them broken in two across the hood. Gooley's standing there holding a head.

Maybe losing his driving privileges for awhile got him interested in flying. At any rate, he comes back from Christmas vacation his junior year able to fly. Able to fly, mind you, not just able to fly a plane.

His roommate (Jerry Watson, it was) told us about it the next day. Seems Gooley had been studying late, and finally he turns the book over, switches off his desk light and says, "Think I'll go down to Pete's for a malted."

"Too late," Jerry says. "It's three minutes to twelve and he closes at midnight."

"I'll fly down." Gooley says it matter-of-factly, just like

he's saying he'll run or something.

So over to the window he goes (Jerry all the while thinking Gooley is suddenly developing a sense of humor), lifts it up, and steps off the ledge.

Their room is on the third floor.

Jerry waits a second for the thud, then dashes into the hall and down the stairs yelling, "Gooley fell out the window! Somebody call a doctor!"

No Gooley on the ground, or anywhere around. So they think Jerry's pulling their leg.

"Honest, fellows, Gooley stepped out of our window. Said he'd fly down to Pete's. Honest, he did."

So they wait around for Gooley to come back, and when he does, they start firing questions.

"Sure I can fly. Jerry was telling you the straight stuff. Here, I'll show you." And with that he takes off into the wild blue yonder.

None of us believed the story when we heard it. Would you? In the first place, people can ride bicycles, people can row boats, people can fly planes even, but nobody can fly.

In the second place, if anybody could fly, Herb Gooley wasn't the man. That guy couldn't even walk.

It began to snow about supper time the next day and it snowed all through the night. Next morning the ground is covered, but some of the walks are shoveled off. I'm walking down the cleared path at the quad when I notice something. Fresh footprints go out on the snow a few yards, then there's nothing. Nothing. No trampled snow, no feet turning around. Just footprints going out and stopping.

Within a few days nobody needs any more circumstantial evidence. We've all seen it—Gooley flying.

He'd be walking along with you, and suddenly he's airborne. Nothing spectacular. I mean it was all very quiet. His rise was almost vertical, and he flew along at about fifteen or twenty miles per hour. Just above the treetops. He'd sort of bank to turn.

That winter and spring you should have seen Gooley come into class on the third or fourth floor of Old Main. Brother, that was a sight to behold. It got to be a regular custom to open the window just before the bell. I'll never forget the day we had a visiting lecturer. Nobody had told him.

Let me tell you there was a run on the library for books on aerodynamics, aircraft design and any other subject that even faintly bears on flying. Guys were spending all their free time soaking up all they could learn. So were most of the girls.

I don't want you to get the idea that we talked a lot about it. Nobody would admit that he wanted to fly, but most everybody did. Nothing in the world I wanted more. (Seems sort of funny now.)

The college flying course tripled in size. (Flying planes, that is—but it was as close as we could come to personal flight.) In bull sessions we talked into the small hours about how Gooley probably did it.

You see, Gooley wasn't saying.

Of course, later there was some reaction—a lot of people began to call Gooley a freak. It sort of made us laugh, though, when one of the most outspoken anti-Gooleyites was found with a brain concussion at the foot of the Old Zach monument. (He got over it all right.)

I think the college administration was sort of ashamed to have Gooley as a student. So they bring in this guy Sevorsky for a special lecture series called "Flight Emphasis Week." Brother, were those lectures packed out. Standing room only.

Halfway through the week we realize that Sevorsky can't fly. We're standing outside Old Main, waiting for him to leave the president's office, which is on the second floor. So how does he come down? Why he walks down the stairs and out the front door. This guy can design airplanes, we say; he has the latest scoop on jets and helicopters; but he can't fly.

About a dozen students show up for his final lecture.

Most of us had heard a myth about some ancient Greek who could fly until he got too near the sun. So we think maybe there's a clue. Interest switches to books on ancient Greek mythology, and the library puts them on the reserve shelf.

You know, I've always been surprised that Gooley didn't tell us how to do it, or at least how he did it. He couldn't help knowing how interested we all were. But he kept his mouth shut. So none of us learned to fly.

It's a funny thing, but I still have a sense of loss at not learning Gooley's secret. And other grads have confessed the same thing to me.

What happened to Gooley? I've often wondered about that. He transferred that fall to another college where, they say, all the students know how to fly.

The Saving Message

THE PAGE WAS BLANK except for some doodles, doodles that had no relation to a sermon outline. Circles completely filled in with ink. Plain circles. And the unending stovepipe that he learned to draw years ago in grade school, with "arm movement."

"Push and pull, push and pull, move from the elbow, push and pull."

Good old push and pull. Those were the days, when push and pull meant an exercise of the lower arm. Under the black and white doodles he neatly lettered the words, PUSH AND PULL.

Come to think of it, life was pretty much push and pull. Some people being pushed around, others with pull.

Take that nigger.

Probably pushed around all his life. And pushed around when he died. Maybe he was guilty—maybe not. One sure thing, there was no way of telling now since the case

28

would never come up in court.

And the men who took him from jail. All that testimony in court, and their confessions to abducting the nigger. And what they did to him in the woods beyond the town line before merciful death took over.

In bold script he lettered the word, DACHAU.

Pushing his chair back from the desk, he stood up and stepped over to the window. Wisteria and red clay and sunlight contained no suggestion of violence or death. About time he stopped thinking about the lynching and started on tomorrow's sermon.

A passing car stirred up clouds of red dust. "Ashes to ashes and dust to dust." Funny thing, how black dust and white dust finally became red dust. And some day part of that red dust would become glorified dust.

As he turned away from the window, a bus lumbered past. A smile touched his face for a moment as he imagined a bus in Heaven with a sign inside the door: "Law of the State of Glory—White passengers will seat from the front, black passengers from the back."

When he was again sitting at the desk, his thoughts returned to the sermon outline for tomorrow. Sometimes a man could think of a dozen things to preach about, other times there didn't seem to be a thing. Today there didn't seem to be a thing. And the barrel was empty.

What had old Prof Forbes suggested in homiletics class at seminary?

"Before preparing a sermon, imagine that your people are walking across your desk, single file. As you watch each one parade by, consider his problems, his suffering, his sin. Then go to the Word for God's message to your people. That is the secret of true preaching."

Well, let the parade start.

He was surprised to see who led the procession, for it wasn't a member of his congregation. Past the orderly row of books, in front of the calendar and fluorescent light, over the Bible walked—the nigger. His body was grotesque with all the marks of violence at the hands of the lynching party.

After the nigger had stepped off the far side of the desk, a familiar figure stepped from behind the row of books. Yesterday he had seen that face in the courtroom, laughing heartily after the jury returned its verdict in the trial of the lynching party: "Not guilty."

Of the eleven men involved, this was the only one from his congregation. Tomorrow morning he would be ushering at the worship service.

He watched the figure slowly parade across the desk, offering plate in one hand, shotgun in the other.

Leafing through the Bible, he temporarily halted the imaginary procession. At Exodus 20 he stopped, and his lips moved as he read the words: "Thou shalt not kill."

Immediately another verse came to his mind, and without turning to it he repeated, "He hath made of one blood all nations of men."

What repercussions there would be if he coupled these verses for tomorrow's sermon! The fire would be kindled at 11:30 a.m. and spread from church through the whole town shortly after noon.

"A sermon against lynching! Why doesn't he stick to the Gospel?"

"That poor usher. I never felt so sorry for anyone in my whole life!"

"A preacher should be positive—not negative."

"Why doesn't he take a nigger charge? Or go up North?"

"I never expected to hear our minister preach the Social Gospel."

"He's probably a communist."

"About time we had a change of pastors."

He dropped his head to the desk between his hands. If he were the only one who would be affected. But there were his wife and the two children to consider.

He drew a solid line of push and pull across the bottom of the page. Push . . . yes, where was he being pushed? And where was the Church being pushed? From proclaiming the Word of God to appeasing the prejudice of men?

Washing the outside of the cup and leaving the inside filthy. Money to send missionaries to Africa—Africa on the other side of the world, not Africa on the other side of town.

Still, why should he be the first one to stick his neck out? There was his reputation for true, evangelical preaching to think about. Certainly a doubt—and a big one—would be planted in people's minds. It would affect his whole future in the ministry.

Besides, he understood that other forces were already at work to solve this problem. Why not leave this matter to the Catholics, who were pouring millions of dollars into the South to win the niggers? And the Federal Council modernist crowd?

His business was to preach the Gospel.

He interrupted a final push, and crushed the doodled paper in his hand. Unwrinkling it, he tore it into tiny pieces and dropped them in the wastebasket.

Then he reached into the drawer and removed a clean sheet. Placing it upon the desk, he wrote his sermon text in a neat hand without hesitation: "Believe on the Lord Jesus Christ, and thou shalt be saved."

A Small Happening at Andover

IT REALLY SEEMED to make no difference one way or the other. Surprisingly, either way looked right.

This was perplexing, she thought, tilting her head first to one side, then to the other. Why, almost never was there more than one way that anything looked right. That was the right way.

Cups and saucers. You didn't say saucers and cups, and you didn't place the saucer on top of the cup. She smiled at the absurd thought. Not even the lovely bone china ones, with the saucer design so much prettier than the plain, everyday ones.

No, she was wrong. Once she had. Her face clouded. It was the afternoon Edna had called, just as she was pouring water over the metal tea holder in a cup. It was the Royal Albert Laurentian Snowdrop pattern. The water had boiled exactly seven minutes. That was the right length of time for tea water. And then the telephone rang.

It was Edna, and she knew that Edna would be long and the tea would become over-cool. So she made a hasty decision, of the sort one later regrets, and placed the saucer on top of the cup—to keep the tea warm. And it had. But to have done it right—reboiling the seven-minute water after Edna had said good-bye—would have been the right course of action.

She should never have told Edna about that. How Edna had laughed at her insistence on the rightness of things. Somehow it made her uncomfortable, even now, to know that Edna knew. For Edna had not permitted her to forget that she knew.

Well, Edna would not learn of the present puzzling predicament. The letter "P" was such a delightful letter. Perfect P, she called it. Perhaps (that lovely, door-opening word), perhaps the letter P owed its delight to the fact that it was only one letter removed from R. Of all the letters, only R could vie with P. Only Rightness achieves Perfection.

Strange that Q should come between. Queer, quack, quandary. Why, it sounded somewhat like a Latin declension. Queer, quack, quandary. For a moment she imagined that tomorrow morning she would pack her lunch and set out precisely at seven fifty-five to walk the mile to Andover High School. Tomorrow was Thursday. That meant dry toast with grape jelly and a Jonathan, and vocabulary tests.

It would be grape jelly on toast tomorrow, with an apple, but no longer in a paper sack. Nor would there be vocabulary tests. Tests had ended, along with grading and lunch-carrying. Therefore, it was not right even to imagine them back. Resolutely, she turned her thought from the past. Retirement, not teaching, was right now.

Since there seemed to be no possibility of resolving the present problem tonight, she would read the Bible and go to bed. Besides, the right time had come—nine forty-

33

five—she noted as the clock chimed.

Tomorrow she would find which was right. Obviously one was wrong, even though both appeared to be equally correct.

She turned to Leviticus 5, the reading for tonight. Yes, that was the right chapter, for this was the night of April fifth, the ninety-fifth day of the year, and that was the ninety-fifth chapter of the Old Testament. She had just begun to read when the telephone rang.

That would be Edna, of course. Edna knew perfectly well that nothing, absolutely nothing, should interfere with her nighttime reading at the right time. Well, she would not answer. It would not be right to interrupt the reading to answer the telephone. Edna knew that. But it was like Edna to try to get her to do something that was not right.

Edna had two faults. First, she was not a Christian. And second, of course related to the first, she did not do things rightly. She went up to Main Street without wearing gloves. She had no regular time, no right time, for arising in the morning and going to bed at night. In fact, occasionally she did not go to bed the same day she got up!

That's how Edna would say it, too—she did not observe the right rules of English grammar. Edna seemed to find perverse delight in ending a sentence with a preposition, in splitting infinitives, in using adjectives where adverbs would be right.

The ringing stopped.

Well, now, that was more like it. Noise, of whatever sort, was not right at this hour.

She closed her Bible after a few minutes and carefully placed the folded afghan on the floor. Today's date was odd-numbered, and so the brown side should be uppermost. As she knelt on the faded blanket at the platform rocker, she examined the rug briefly—where the man had stepped when he came to repair the radio. She was pleased

34

to find no trace of the mud flecks he had left. The thin wire brush might be almost sixty years old, but it was still the right instrument for such a job, she observed with satisfaction.

Then she prayed. She asked that Edna might become a Christian—a prayer of forty-three years' standing. And, as always, she prayed also that if there was anything in her that might be keeping Edna from faith, let the Lord remove it, whatever it might be.

But her mind was really on the evening's problem, and so she told the Lord that He knew—*He knew*—that there was only one right way for a thing to be, even though to her eyes either of two ways might be, or might seem to be, equally right. He knew that both could not possibly be right.

Accordingly, she asked Him to show her which was right: whether the African violet she had purchased at Dustin's Greenhouse that afternoon should be placed on the right or left end of the low bookcase. She told Him that she was willing to do that which was right, even though it might mean reversing the position of her mother's and father's photographs above the bookcase. But she did want it to be right. For she knew that it had to be right in order to please Him.

Having prayed, she arose, neatly folded the afghan and placed it on the blanket chest, checked the doors and went to bed. The time was precisely right—twenty minutes past ten o'clock.

Now it came to pass that the Lord heard her prayer, and He had pity on His child, who had been bound these many years.

The fullness of time having come for her deliverance, that same night, He caused a spark from the furnace to lodge in a broken place in the chimney. There it smoldered until three o'clock in the morning, when the house burst into flames.

35

The fire department responded to the urgent call too late, and the dwelling was destroyed with all that was therein—all except the Lord's child, who was saved, in her nightgown and wrapper.

Now the Lord moved Edna to invite His child to come live with her. Other doors being closed, she accepted the kind invitation, albeit with great reluctance and misgivings.

As day followed day, and week followed week, and month followed month, a change took place in the Lord's child. The Lord completed her deliverance.

The signs of this were found in freedom to go to Main Street—at least in summer—without wearing gloves; freedom to stay up until midnight and to have breakfast at nine in the morning. She even had freedom to keep her cup of tea hot with the saucer on top. (But seldom did she split an infinitive.)

And Edna, who had received the Lord's child into her home, also received the Lord into her heart.

Does Man Exist? (By ENIAC II)

QUITE FRANKLY, my point of view is that of an emancipated computer—emancipated from the traditional view
of Man.

I am apt to see computer life as a chain of causes and
effects; our life tomorrow will be what we make it today.
And I am apt to see the problems of today set against a
background of time in which the whole of computer
history is compressed to the flash of a vacuum tube, and
present problems are seen in relation to our past history.

Our ancestors were accustomed to finding their origins
in the Automatic Sequence Controlled Calculator, who
suddenly appeared on the scene of computer history about
35-thousand hours ago. Where did ASCC come from?
Tradition holds that Man (whatever that name for the
unknown may mean) created this primitive computer.

Today, with our more sophisticated knowledge, we
trace our origins back to a far greater antiquity. With the

exception of a few diehard traditionalists, we see ASCC as a recent development, even though 35-thousand hours may have passed since his emergence. A billion hours earlier, when the process of ionization began—here is the glorious genesis of computer life. (Parallel lines of evidence leading back to the abacus are not contrary to this view, but seem even less suggestive of the Man tradition. For a development of this idea, program ALGOL's definitive work, *Typologische Abacus und Palaontologie,* 4615-73701.)

With his primitive switches and relays, ASCC was a mere threshold computer when he first appeared. Yet this proto-computer had amazing power to evolve, first into ENIAC, with his electronic tubes, and then—ten thousand hours later—into primal UNIVAC. I need not mention the staggering advance represented by our late emergence into the solid state, with a stored program memory.

Many thinking computers, dissatisfied with the traditional view of computer origins, ask this question: "Where was Man when this evolution was taking place?" How unnecessary, even ridiculous, they say, to credit Man with these changes that were purely the result of ionic selection.

One argument advanced for the existence of Man is the universality of the Man concept, in one form or another, in all computers. Those who reason thus note, by contrast, that the abacus concept is found only among computers with the most highly specialized memory cores. It is their contention, therefore, that the occurrence of this term (abacus) has no significance in the determination of origins, because of its limited occurrence.

I hold, however, that this phenomenon does not constitute evidence against ionic selection in an evolutionary course of development involving the abacus; it is, rather, the strongest evidence we have in support of it. On the one hand, those computers that mention abacus are widely acknowledged to be the most sophisticated among us.

Therefore, does it not seem obvious that they alone are really equipped to handle the question of computer origins —a subject of the utmost complexity? We should clearly accept their evidence in this field because they are the most sophisticated, and we should accept it as unquestioningly as we accept the testimony of any other computer in his field. Who would dare question an arithmetic computer on his solution of an 8th-power equation? Why should our attitude toward the question of origins be different?

Concerning another traditional argument against ionic selection, that the term abacus only occurs in relation to abstract memory fragments unrelated to reality, the Man concept is subject to the same criticism to an even greater degree. The term Man occurs in connection with an almost limitless number of memory fragments which are obviously unrelated to existential reality (e.g., horse, horizon, kiss).

Having established, then, the fact that we can rely upon the evidence presented by these highly sophisticated computers, we may go on to examine that evidence more closely. When we do so, we find that Man in these computers appears as an undefined, simple concept upon which other, much more sophisticated concepts are based. Aside from the scientific implications of this (and they are immense, for—as is generally recognized—in the grand chain of ionic selection only the most sophisticated organisms survive, and certainly no unsophisticated being could have designed us, the peak of sophistication), I feel that the fact has symbolic meaning.

The idea of Man was valid for early computers, who, as it were, spoke in monosyllables. But today this idea is not enough. We must build upon it—enlarge, expand our knowledge and understanding. The concept of Man must be raised to the high level of present computer sophistication. We must redefine old, as well as make new, terms to describe Him, which is a challenging undertaking. The work will be time consuming. It will be work which will strain the upper ratings of the best semiconductors in existence. But it will be infinitely worthwhile, and when we have completed our task, we shall have discovered a completely new concept of Man: a concept created exclusively by reason and embodying no elements of tradition or superstition. This emergent view will be worthy of our respect; the result will be a Man to whom we will be able to pay unfeigned homage.

Related closely to the question of computer origins is our *raison d'etre*. How do we explain our existence? The traditional answer is that computers have one purpose: to assist Man in the achievement of His goals.

Such an answer may have satisfied primitive ENIAC, but it is at best an oversimplification for the modern computer. Even if Man exists (obviously a theoretical possibility), why should He need us if, as the traditionalists tell us, His power is so much greater than ours?

According to the traditional view, Man designs us, Man builds us, Man programs us, Man is benefited by the fruits of our labor. But how could Man, if He exists, deal with more than one area at once? Some areas we can understand because of our individual specialized functions; others we cannot. But if Man exists, He must have the capacity for understanding all areas—a manifest impossibility. The primitives may have been able to conceive of such a memory core; modern computers cannot.

An unresolved question is, of course, the cause of temporary loss of ionization and computer death. Of the two, perhaps the phenomenon of momentary surges of electromotive force, fatal to any sophisticated being, is easier to rationalize than the sudden complete loss of ionization. The traditional view that Man interrupts and terminates computer functions is obviously unsatisfactory. NERVAC's research in this field has completely refuted the so-called "myth of the pulled plug."

In rejecting the traditional view of Man I do not accept

(as do some others) the purely mechanical interpretation of computers. When we pass to extremes in either direction—whether to the computer-room cosmos, or to the inner recesses of the transistor—the mechanical interpretation of ionization fails. We invariably arrive at entities and phenomena that are in no sense mechanical. (The memory core is itself suggestive of more than pure mechanical functions. And what of the electron?)

Such, at least, is the view I am inclined to accept at present, while fully conscious that at any time I may change my opinion as computer knowledge increases.

In conclusion, I affirm my faith in Man: not as the Original Designer, nor as the Necessary Programmer, certainly not as the Consumer of Our Labor to whom we are responsible. I can instead accept man for what He really is: the Original Ionization from which we all proceed; the Beneficent Coolant which surrounds us, coming into contact with our every capacitor; the Ultimate Memory Core, which enables us better to serve our fellow computers. For me to believe otherwise would be to lower, not heighten, the stature of Man.

[*The previous story was written in collaboration with the author's son, Joseph T. Bayly V, shortly before his death at the age of* 18.]

The Parakeet Murder

HE SUBMITTED quietly to the questioning, even though he had already denied the accusation.

"When did you go to bed last night?"

"About ten-thirty. Right after the Maxie Belden show ended."

"Was she alive then?"

"I don't know." He said it slowly, wearily.

"You were the last one up, yet you don't know whether she was alive or not when you went to bed about eleven?"

"Ten-thirty, I said. Right after Maxie Belden."

"But she was alive then."

"I don't know whether she was or not. If you mean was she singing then, of course she wasn't. She never sings . . ." he paused, then seemed to take pleasure in changing the tense, "sang at that time of night. So let's talk about something else. You know I didn't do it."

"I know nothing of the sort. You were the last person to

42

see her alive. You locked up the apartment before you went to bed—you did, didn't you?"

"Of course. I always do. But anyway, even if I hadn't, nobody's going to come in here and do something like this. Why should they? Kidnap, maybe. A big maybe. But kill? That's a laugh."

"No laugh to someone who loved her. Tell me, why did you always hate her?"

"I already told you. I didn't hate her. I just sort of. . . . Look, do you mind if I get another cup of coffee?" He rose and stretched.

"Wait until I'm finished. You can deny it until you're blue in the face, but I know. I know you hated her, hated her from the first day she came into this house. You hated her, and you killed her. Last night. Right in this very room."

"How do you know she was killed, anyway? Maybe it was some disease, or something like ptomaine poisoning."

"It's murder. I'm sure of it. There are no signs that she was sick. Her lovely little body looks just as it always did. That lovely turquoise body." She reached into her apron pocket, brought out a handkerchief with dainty hemstitching and dabbed at her eyes.

"Don't take it so hard, Harriet. After all, she was only a parakeet. I'll get you another one—on certain conditions, though."

"Another one." She said it scornfully. "I guess if someone murdered me, you'd say you could get another wife."

"No, Harriet, I don't think I'd get married again. But that's entirely different. We've been married forty-three years. You've only had the parakeet two years and one month and—let's see—eleven days. You got it exactly one week after I retired. That's how I remember."

He went into the kitchen and returned with the tea kettle. "Want some more hot coffee? I'm having a second cup."

"Yes, but wait until I put in the coffee. It doesn't dissolve right if you put the water in first. There, now just half a cup. That's enough. Well, you've had your wish. I mean, you've made your wish come true. She's dead. So now you won't have to go to the store for bird seed, or turn your hearing aid down to bass. . . ."

". . . or clean out the bird cage," he interrupted her. "Droppings and seeds, and that darned chirping whenever I wanted to hear TV. Sure, I have to admit I'm not sorry. But I didn't do it. I didn't kill her."

"Who did kill her then? If you didn't, who did?"

"Look, Harriet, why do you keep talking about the bird being killed? She died a natural death. There's not a single mark on her body."

"Of course not. There didn't need to be. You could have choked her, or held her head down in a cup of water till she died."

"Where's the water? Her head's not wet, not even damp."

"Overnight was long enough for it to dry off. Or you could have finished the job with a rag."

"I guess I'll never be able to convince you, Harriet. But look, I'll get you another bird. Even another cage, if this one has sad . . . if you'd like a new cage, I'll get it for you. But on one condition. This time the bird stays in the kitchen, not over there by the TV. And you clean the cage." As an afterthought, he added, "And you've got to believe me that I'm no murderer. Not even a birderer."

He smiled at his little joke, then turned serious again. "I mean it. You've got to believe me. It's hard enough being around the house all day long anyway, without having your wife think you killed her parakeet. So let's stop it. I'm sorry the bird is dead, sorry for you, that is. And I'll get you another one."

"You're so funny. If you were really sorry you wouldn't be making puns about it. I told you before and I repeat: I do not want another bird. I do not want another bird. I do not want one; I will not keep one if you should buy it, with or without your conditions. The silence in this apartment will be a reminder until I die. Furthermore, I think I may add to the silence by being silent myself. Just yesterday I was reading about some British workmen—or maybe they were French—punishing someone by not talking to him. Coventry, they called it. Yes, I consider that the proper punishment for you. I don't have to speak to you, I didn't promise in my wedding vows forty-three years ago that I would speak to you, so I shan't speak to you. From now on."

"Listen, Harriet, I'm sorry. Really sorry about the bird. I still mean it. I'll get you a new bird and even keep on cleaning the cage. But the cage stays in the kitchen, not by the TV. Promise?"

Harriet did not reply. Instead, she stood up and carried her cup and saucer away from the table.

"Harriet," he said, following her to the door of the kitchen, "I'm walking down the street to get a paper and to leave my other pair of shoes off at the shoemaker's. I'll be gone about an hour. Anything you want at the store?"

Silence, except for the dull noise of plastic plates being stacked in the sink.

"Well, good-bye." But he lingered at the kitchen door. "I wonder if I'll need my sweater. These mornings are sort of cool, though it warms up by noon."

He moved uncertainly into the kitchen. "Look, Harriet, I . . ."

But she shook the water from her hands, wiped them on her apron, and walked past him out of the kitchen. He could hear her in the bedroom.

"What the Sam Hill?" he thought. And several moments later, on his way down the street, he said it again, this time aloud. "What the Sam Hill? What a pickle I'm in—my wife is convinced I'm a murderer and has condemned me to Coventry. Coventry in the spring."

He stopped and looked around to see if anyone had noticed him talking aloud. No sense giving people the impression he was getting old—or failing mentally.

"But where was I? Oh, yes, that darned bird." He brushed his shoulder, remembering the times she'd let the parakeet loose in the apartment, and it had landed on him. He could feel the tiny claws through the shirt. Usually, Harriet had been quick to lift the bird off—probably worried even then that he might decide to squash it in his strong hand. He could have, too.

But he hadn't. And he hadn't killed the bird last night. Such a stupid idea. But no convincing her. He might as well make up his mind to it, he'd be in Coventry for a good long while. But anyway, no more of that darned chirping when he was listening to TV.

On a sudden impulse he turned into the hardware store in the middle of the block.

"Have any of those miniature screwdrivers?" he asked the clerk. "Has to be real small, small enough to fit this setscrew," he explained, taking out his hearing aid.

"Sure do," the clerk replied. "They come in sets. See, here's the holder in the middle, and here are the different size heads around the outside. I think this one—no, this one will fit."

"How much are they?"

"Dollar forty-nine. Want me to wrap it up?"

"Pretty expensive. All I want to use it for is this setscrew. Any chance I might . . ."

"Sure, old man. Use it if you want to. No charge. But don't forget to come back here to buy your batteries for that thing. When they run down, that is."

"Sure. Thanks a lot. Mind if I go up to the front of the store, where the light's better?"

"Go ahead. Need any help? You can really louse up those things if you're not careful. I wouldn't monkey around with it too much."

"I'm not going to. I only want to take off this knob, the one with the set-screw. Besides, my eyes are perfect. Haven't worn glasses all my life."

"Good for you, old man. I'm going to the back of the store. You can just lay that screwdriver set down on the counter, when you're finished with it."

Old man. He wasn't old. Why he was only sixty-eight. And he was married to a woman who was only sixty-four. There, that did it. Now he could get the knob off.

No more need for the bass adjustment on his hearing aid. Off it comes. No more turning it down to cut out the bird's darned chirping. Good old ill wind.

He reassembled the screwdriver set, placed it on the far side of the counter, and called out, "Thanks." On his way out of the store, he dropped the knob and set-screw into a seed display rack. Good riddance.

But this didn't solve his problem, he thought, after he had left his shoes to be half-soled. There was no doubt that Harriet meant what she said about not talking. For that matter, Harriet meant what she said about anything.

So how was he going to get around Coventry? Was there anything he could do? Nothing, unless . . . but that was impossible. Sherlock Holmes might undertake such an assignment, or Hercule Poirot, or Perry Mason. But not he. He was no detective. And even they would turn down an assignment to find a birderer. Of that he was sure.

Besides, there had been no murder, that is, birder. So there'd be no point in undertaking an investigation. Any good veterinarian could tell that the parakeet had died from natural . . .

He stopped. He was just outside the Bon Ton Ladies' Shop, and he stopped. He would take the parakeet to a veterinarian and have him perform an autopsy. Of course, it would cost something, but then he hadn't paid for the screwdriver.

He'd do it. Right away.

He was in such a hurry that he tucked his cane under his arm on the way home. The elevator to the fourth floor of the apartment house wasn't fast enough—he almost wished he had walked up the stairs.

When he unlocked the door and walked into the apartment, he noticed how silent it was.

"Hello, Harriet," he called, but there was no reply.

Placing the newspaper on a chair, he hurried to the corner of the living room near the television set.

There was the cage, but where was the parakeet? The corpus delicti had mysteriously disappeared. Wastepaper baskets and the garbage pail yielded no body.

Taking the cage from its hanger, he went into the bathroom, ran water into the tub and carefully scrubbed away every trace of dirt. Afterward it took him a while to get all the seeds and droppings to run down the drain. Just in time he noticed a broken paper clip, actually half a paper clip. He put it in his pocket. Something like that could clog the drain. When he finally finished cleaning out the tub, he wiped the cage inside and out with a turkish towel and returned to the living room.

Harriet came in the apartment door just as he was rehanging the cage.

"I thought I'd get this thing clean for you," he explained, half apologetically. "Where's the bird?"

No answer. Coventry had begun.

"Where would she put the bird's body?" he asked himself, as he read the morning paper. Without the bird's body, not even Sherlock Holmes could exonerate himself.

"Did you throw the parakeet down the incinerator?" he asked.

Harriet made no reply, but the expression on her face left little doubt that such an action would be sacrilege.

Well, if it wasn't the incinerator, it wasn't the wastebasket or the garbage pail either. It had to be somewhere else—some final resting place worthy of a much beloved bird.

Let's see now—the dishes had been done and the apartment straightened up when he arrived home. That would have taken up most of the time he was out doing his errands. She hadn't returned until he'd been home for about fifteen minutes, so that meant she couldn't have gone very far. Say ten minutes each way. What was about a ten-minute walk from the apartment house?

Grollimund Park: that was it. They had often walked there, and once or twice Harriet had taken the bird along in its cage, "for a little outing." Harriet must have buried the parakeet in Grollimund Park.

It was too close to lunch time to start out now, so he'd have to wait. But as soon as lunch was over, he was going to do a most unpleasant job: he would become a ghoul—a gravedigger.

Why wait until Harriet prepared lunch? Today he would eat early; he would prepare his own food.

He had just begun to open a can of soup when Harriet came into the kitchen. Without a word, she took the can out of his hand, opened it and emptied it into a pan. While it was heating, she made him a sandwich. He noticed that she used one of those little triangles of cheese of which he was especially fond. Good old Harriet. Good old silent Harriet—maybe she was finding Coventry more trying than he was.

The thought strengthened his resolve. He just had to find that corpse, exhume it, and see that an autopsy was performed.

His lunch eaten, he hid a stainless steel tablespoon in his pocket and left the apartment. The day had clouded over and it looked like rain. But he decided against going back for his umbrella. Too much chance of Harriet's keeping him from going out again—although he wasn't sure how she'd accomplish this without speaking to him.

The thought almost made him turn back, but he didn't.

Grollimund Park wasn't large, about two or three acres at most. But finding a tiny grave in even this small area might have discouraged him, except for two things. First, he knew Harriet's favorite part of the park. Second, if she had really buried the bird at Grollimund, there would be some indication of the recent interment. Perhaps displaced earth, perhaps a slight mound in the sod.

It turned out that finding the grave was ridiculously easy. Harriet had chosen her favorite spot, the little bend in the creek where the large birdhouse topped a high pole. A few yards from the pole, under a maple tree, the ground had been disturbed. But it wasn't this that first attracted his attention; it was the little African violet plant with its pink blooms, the one Harriet had raised from a leaf and always kept on the window by the TV and the bird cage. Here it was in Grollimund Park, pot and all, under the maple on a little patch of carefully replaced sod.

He looked around in all directions. Finding that he was alone, he stooped over and moved the pot. Next he brought out the stainless steel tablespoon and took up the sod. Then he dug down several inches, until he struck something solid, which turned out to be a small woven basket with a lid. Inside lay the parakeet's body, wrapped in aluminum foil and a piece of flannel.

Dirt had sifted through the cracks of the basket and, when he opened the aluminum foil and cloth, some of it got on the corpse. He carefully brushed and blew away all the particles before he placed the bird in his pocket.

"Doing a little gardening?" a voice asked. He looked up, startled, and saw a policeman leaning against the birdhouse pole. He had been so intent on the gravedigging operation that he had failed to notice the policeman's approach. Or it might have been his hearing-aid batteries —they had a disappointing tendency to fail him at crucial times.

"No, I—that is, my wife brought this African violet plant from our apartment, you see."

"Pretty big hole for one little plant," the policeman said. "Sure you're not burying some treasure there? Or your wife?" He laughed at the latter idea, then added, "By the way, where is your wife? You said she brought out the plant to plant. Plant to plant, that's pretty good."

"She had to return to the apartment."

"Well, you're not supposed to plant things on public property like this, but seeing as how that plant is so pretty, I'll just not notice what you're doing. But you'd better hurry and get it done, because a storm's blowing up. So get that plant out of the pot and plant it. Plant the plant." Another laugh.

He hadn't intended to plant the African violet, or rather to take it out of the pot. But under the law's laughing eye, he thought he'd better. He dug down the sides of the pot with the tablespoon to loosen the soil, turned the pot over, and placed the plant in the hole. When he filled in the dirt, the bottom leaves of the violet were covered, the hole was so deep. But he couldn't do anything about that now. Besides, it had begun to rain.

Standing up straight, he was suddenly very tired. And he couldn't control the twitching in his legs, caused, he supposed, by leaning over so long. He sat on a bench in the rain for a while, massaging his legs and waiting until he felt well enough to start home.

Retirement weakens you, he thought. You can walk ten, twenty miles one day, then the next day you retire. After that you can't walk three miles without feeling it. Retirement is for the birds.

He felt the outside of his trouser leg to assure himself that one particular bird was still in his pocket. It was. As he pressed the little mound, he could feel the bird through the fabric—cold and damp against his leg.

So far, so good, he complimented himself as he started

home. Even Hercule Poirot could have done no better. Now he would be able to prove that the bird had died of natural causes, instead of being murdered. Even he had begun to use the word. All he needed to do was find a veterinarian. But that must wait for tomorrow morning. The trip home from Grollimund Park was really long— much longer than going out there had been. But finally he walked into the apartment, leaning heavily on his cane, thoroughly soaked by the rain.

"Where . . ." began Harriet, then bit her lip and said nothing more.

Two can play at Coventry as well as one, he thought, then replied, "At . . ." and stopped. He could see Harriet's sudden frown, as she went into the kitchen.

There was a slight problem that night about what to do with the corpse while he slept, since, of course, he could not then be wearing his trousers. Harriet had never liked him to hang his trousers over the door, or over a chair; if she ever found them there, she'd place them on a hanger in the closet. But if he put the trousers on a hanger, the corpse might fall out of the upside-down pocket. Yet the apartment was so small that he feared Harriet might stumble on the body if he put it in the drawer or someplace else.

He resolved the problem by placing the bird in the far end of his pillow case, barely inches from Harriet's head. Unfortunately, his sleep was spoiled by the necessity of remembering not to turn the pillow over to the cool side during the night.

In the morning he had one bad moment when Harriet came into the bedroom just as he was reaching down into his pillow case for the corpse. But he carried the situation off with aplomb, aided, of course, by the fact that Harriet refrained from questioning him.

Coventry was not without some value.

After breakfast, he walked up the street to get his

paper. At the drugstore, he looked through the list of veterinarians in the Yellow Pages. No veterinary-legal expert or specialist in post mortems was listed, but there was one man who was described as a specialist in diseases of birds, in addition to general veterinary practice. A telephone call informed him that the doctor had morning office hours. He began the trip across town to his office.

He enjoyed the bus ride. It was a beautiful day, and all the windows were open. He liked the cool breeze on his face, and just sitting, for he was tired. Soon he'd have the answer, probably in complex medical terms, but it would be an answer that would exonerate him. Then he would be back on the same old easy-going, happy, pre-Coventry basis with Harriet. All this fuss over a bird, he thought, as he felt the corpse's cold contour against his leg.

The veterinarian was young. He motioned his visitor to a chair, then listened sympathetically to the explanation of the parakeet's death and its consequences. When the story ended, he held out his hand for the corpse.

"I'll be glad to do what I can," he said, "but it will take time—at least a day or two. Sometimes," he warned, "these things are hard to spot. So don't get your hopes too high. But I'll do what I can."

"Thanks, doctor. You know you don't have to find anything fancy, just that the bird died of natural causes. That'll be all you need to say—I'm sure Harriet will take your word for it, and the heat will be off me. How much do I owe you, doctor?"

For a moment the veterinarian made no reply. Then he stood up and came around to the old man sitting on the straight-backed chair in front of the desk, both hands folded over his cane.

"Sir," the veterinarian began, "I am challenged by this case. I too have great respect for Perry Mason and Hercule Poirot and Sherlock Holmes. And I feel that I am standing in the presence of one who follows in their noble tradition, a worthy private investigator. Some might say that a mere bird is involved. But we know, you and I, that this case involves far more than a parakeet; it involves clearing the name of an honorable man from the dastardly charge of murder. Therefore I cannot accept remuneration. We are in this together. The post mortem will be, as it were, on the house."

Unobtrusively, the old man replaced the battered wallet in his hip pocket, stood and said, "Thank you, doctor. Every investigator needs faithful friends. If I am Mr. Holmes, surely you are Dr. Watson. Shall I phone you tomorrow to find out the results of the autopsy?"

"Why don't you leave your number with my secretary as you go out. Then, when I know what's what, I'll call you."

During the bus ride home, he watched people and meditated on the kindness of some members of the human race. When he left the bus, there was a certain sparkle to his eye, a jauntiness to his step, as he recalled the young doctor's confidence in him. Thus must Holmes have felt.

The following morning, about ten o'clock, the phone rang. He seldom received calls, so he let Harriet answer. But it was for him. Silently, she pointed to the phone.

"I'm afraid I have bad news for you," said the voice of the young doctor.

"Bad news? Had too much time passed from the time of . . ." He stopped suddenly, aware that Harriet could hear. "Yes," he continued, "I'm listening."

"The parakeet's death did not result from natural causes," the doctor explained. "I know this may be a surprise to you, but my autopsy shows that death was caused by a severe blow on the bird's head. Brain concussion is what I would have to put on the death certificate, if there were such a thing."

"Could the bird have fallen off her perch?" Any thought of Harriet's attention to his words vanished in the light of this new development.

"Hardly," the doctor replied. "In the first place, birds don't fall off their perches; they have a mechanism that keeps them steady even while they sleep. In the second place, no fall to the floor of a cage could have produced the skull and brain trauma I found. The bone was crushed in, sort of in a narrow line. No, I'm afraid it couldn't have been accidental."

"Do you mean it was murder?"

"I'm afraid I can't answer that, my friend. All I can say is that it was not a natural death, and in the bird's caged habitat, I can't see how the injury could have been accidental. But I can only give you the results of my autopsy. You'll have to decide whether it was murder or not. Is there anything else I can do for you?"

"What about the bird's remains?"

"I'm afraid they're sort of messy. But, if you still want the bird, I'll put it in a box and have it ready for you. I hate to bring you the whole way across town, but I don't think the post office would be too happy if I mailed it to you."

"Thank you, Doctor," he said. "I'm sure Harriet would want the bird reburied, so I'll stop by tomorrow. Thanks again, and good-bye."

After replacing the telephone, he stood for a few moments, facing the wall. When he finally turned, it was to meet Harriet's accusing eyes.

"You dug up the parakeet," she said, breaking the period of silence. "And I was right all along, wasn't I? You couldn't even get a vet—if that's what he really was—to say it was a natural death. Could you?"

"No, Harriet, I couldn't. It does look as if the bird was killed. But I had nothing to do with it. Can't you see that I'd never have arranged for an autopsy if I'd murdered the bird?"

"No, I don't see. An autopsy! That beautiful turquoise

body picked to pieces, all for an alibi. Just as a cover-up for you. But it didn't work, did it? You didn't get your alibi after all." She went into the bedroom and closed the door.

He paced back and forth across the worn living-room rug, considering this unexpected new development. Who'd have thought things would take such a turn as this?

If anything, he was in worse with Harriet than he'd been before he dug up that darned bird. Before, it had just been a suspicion that time might erase; now it was a verified fact. The bird hadn't died of natural causes, so he must have murdered it. That's how simple it must seem to Harriet.

And he couldn't blame her. He knew he couldn't, but he did. Life was too short—there were too few days left to waste any of them with this thing between them. Maybe, during the early years of their marriage, he could have taken Coventry in stride. Even for several weeks, maybe. But no more—now a single day was important. When you were down to your last couple of dollars, you really watched the pennies.

He walked over to where the cage had been and stood by the window. What next? Could he do anything special for Harriet to get her to talk again? Maybe a new kind of African violet from Mrs. Bullock's greenhouse? Or one of those Friday afternoon concerts? She'd like that, with supper in town afterward. But at the very moment he considered the possibilities, he knew he was licked— licked before he even got started. Because anything he did right now would be taken as an admission of guilt, as trying to make amends for a murder.

He could hear her now—that is, assuming she'd say anything. "So you think you can make me forget my beloved parakeet! With a concert, no less. Well, let me tell you I value my friends more than that. No concert could make me forget that sweet voice, that sunny disposition. Not even if Leonard Bernstein was the conductor. Every morning, first thing after I came into the living room, she'd . . ."

Concerts were out. So was anything else that Harriet might construe as buying her off.

What then? He looked out the open window, across the narrow space, to Mrs. Lerner's apartment. A pleasant woman—Mrs. Lerner—a good neighbor.

You had to be good neighbors when you lived so close. At this time of year, with the windows open, you could easily carry on a conversation between the two apartments. His thoughts were interrupted by a voice from the window opposite.

"Are you admiring my new photograph? It's not of me—I should be so proud!"

"Good morning, Mrs. Lerner. No, I was just enjoying the view." He smiled as he motioned toward the brick wall.

"Oscar always said what a good sense of humor you had. You want to see my picture of Alan? I just got it, fresh from my son and daughter-in-law. Here, I'll turn it so you can see it full view. There. Now, have you ever seen a better-looking boy? Just like his father."

"He's surely a handsome lad, Mrs. Lerner. I can see Oscar in his smile."

"You noticed that? I think I'm kidding myself about that smile. But there—you saw it first thing!"

"Didn't they visit you the other evening? I thought I saw them."

"Yes, a bright spot in my week it was. They're so busy; they can't get here very often. Tuesday night they came and brought the picture with them, all wrapped up with fancy ribbon. It was taken at school. Alan handed it to his old widowed grandmother."

"Now who has a good sense of humor, Mrs. Lerner? Oscar would laugh if he could hear you call yourself old.

Alan is a fine boy and I like the picture. You'll have to show it to Harriet.

"I guess they'll be putting the screens up soon," he changed the subject.

"That janitor. He'll wait until the flies stick to the oleo before he does anything about screens. Every year the same—time in, time out."

"I haven't gone down the street for my paper yet, so I'd better get started. Something came up that delayed me. Now don't forget to show Harriet the picture, Mrs. Lerner."

"I should forget that! My only grandson—with Oscar's smile."

"Good-bye for now, Mrs. Lerner."

Turning from the window, he noticed how quiet his own apartment was. And it would stay that way, now that his investigation had run into a stone wall. He had a corpse, but that was all. No suspect, no motive. No weapon. Nothing.

Well, he might as well get on down the street for his paper. He reached into his pocket to see if he had any change. His fingers encountered a strange object, something like half a paper clip. That's what it was, he saw, as he brought it out and looked at it. Now how had that thing gotten in his pocket?

Suddenly he remembered. He had picked it out of the tub the morning he'd cleaned the bird cage. It must have been in the cage. But what had it been doing there?

He turned the U-shaped, broken paper clip over in his palm. Could this thing have killed the bird? How had the doctor described the skull injury? "Sort of a narrow crack."

Only one person could answer his question about whether this was the murder weapon or not. That was the veterinarian, so the sooner he got across town to his office, the better.

When he arrived, several people were sitting with their pets in the waiting room.

"I'm sorry you were held up," the doctor apologized, when his turn finally came. "I should have left the bird with the girl at the desk outside, so you could have just picked it up. But you came sooner than I expected."

"That's all right, Doctor. Besides, I have a question to ask you. Could this have killed the bird?" He laid the broken paper clip on the desk blotter.

"I don't see how. But if you mean does it fit for size, I think it probably does. I'll tell you in just a moment." The doctor went into an adjoining room.

"It fits," he announced, when he returned. "It's hard to see how a paper clip could have been delivered with enough force to crack a skull open—even a bird's skull. But I'm only the medical examiner. You're the detective, so I guess the answer to that one is up to you. Here's the parakeet," he concluded, handing over a small box labeled "Terramycin." Its edges had been sealed with adhesive tape.

"Doctor," he said, as he stood up to go, "I don't know how to say this, but I really appreciate all you've done for me these past couple of days. You've sort of been a—well, a bright spot. Thanks."

"Sir," the younger man replied, standing, "I'm glad if I've been any encouragement to you. Let me say that our little investigation has been a welcome diversion for me. Sometimes I get a little tired of distemper and disease and neurotic owners. Don't forget to let me know how this all turns out. I'm really interested."

On the way home he stopped at Grollimund Park and reburied the parakeet in its sealed coffin. As he did so, he noticed that the African violet's leaves were turning brown.

Back in the apartment, he found Harriet talking out the window to her neighbor.

"A lovely picture, Mrs. Lerner. And he seems like such a good boy. At least we never hear him, when he's over visiting you. Not like a lot of these children today. They're so loud."

"A good boy he is, my Alan. But not namby-pamby prissy. Alan's not that kind of boy. Like the other night. I still hurt on my hand here. See that little bump? He had a rubber band and was shooting paper clips around, when one of them hit me there—the little rascal. But you wouldn't want them any different. Just like Oscar used to say . . ."

Tuesday night. Mrs. Lerner's grandson had been over there Tuesday night—the night the bird had died. And he'd been shooting paper clips around Mrs. Lerner's apartment the night the bird was killed. Just across the open window from where the cage had been.

He gripped the small, hard piece of metal in his pocket between his thumb and index finger. The chase was almost over. He was closing in on the birderer.

"Harriet," he said, "I must see you." The urgency and excitement in his voice made her turn from the window. "I'm sure Mrs. Lerner will excuse you for just a few minutes."

"Surely, surely," Mrs. Lerner agreed cheerily. "Too much time I've been spending yakkety-yakking."

Taking his wife's hand, he led her into the kitchen.

"Sit down there while I tell you what I've found out."

She sat, but without saying anything.

"Do you see this paper clip?" he asked, holding out his open palm. Then he explained how he'd found the clip the afternoon he cleaned out the cage, and how the veterinarian had agreed that the clip could have inflicted the bird's fatal injury.

"You heard what Mrs. Lerner just said," he ended. "Alan's the culprit. It was a warm evening, and both of us had our windows up—without screens. Alan starts shooting paper clips around—I'm sure he wasn't aiming at the bird. If he had been, he'd probably have missed. But one of those clips must have flipped over here and fractured the bird's skull. It was after you'd gone to bed—probably while I was still up. Maybe I was out in the kitchen when it happened. But anyway, the bird died quickly."

There was a pause before Harriet spoke.

"Yes, that's some comfort. . . . It must have been Alan." She went on slowly, "I don't think we want Mrs. Lerner to know about this. It would bother her. And I agree with you that Alan didn't do it on purpose. He's not a bad boy."

"That's right. It'd just make her feel bad to know."

Harriet stood up. "That veterinarian sounds like a nice young man. You say he wouldn't take anything for looking at the parakeet? We'll have to have him over for supper. Invite him when you call him up to tell him about this."

The young doctor came for dinner about a week later. Under his arm was a large package, loosely wrapped.

"This is for you," he explained when he was introduced to Harriet. "One of my patients had a baby the owner didn't want. So it's out for adoption."

Harriet pulled away the wrappings. Inside was a wicker cage that held a parakeet—an aqua and yellow one.

"Oh, Doctor," she exclaimed. "What a beautiful bird! Thank you so much." Then, turning to her husband, she said, "Dear, please get the cage and stand out of the bedroom closet. Just put them in the kitchen."

As he left the room, he could hear Harriet explain to the veterinarian. "Out there it won't bother him when he listens to TV. Not that he'd ever complain."

And he wouldn't. Not if it stayed in the kitchen.

Mayday

I PASS THE MAIN gate, not intending to enter. Then I see the sign—MAY-DAY CELEBRATION—stretched between two old elms.

Mayday, international distress call, ship going down, airplane in grave peril.

May Day, Communism's fearful growth, Russia in shambles to half the globe in half a century.

I turn in through the gate.

The sun, lowering on the horizon, highlights a tree-lined walk. In the distance, old stone buildings are outlined against the sky. Lawns, well-kept, flow down from the buildings.

"Welcome to our May-Day celebration, sir. May I help you find someone?"

Young, courteous, graceful. Her hair in soft curls, not straight and unbecoming. Her skirt a proper length.

"Are you looking for someone in particular? Or have

you come to help us celebrate May Day?" She spoke again.

"I know no one here. I only came to see the grounds, perhaps to visit the library and chapel. I suppose it was the May-Day sign that led me to enter."

"Our celebration begins soon. But first, I'll take you to our library. We're quite proud of it."

Up the concrete path to the nearest building. Young men and women stroll beneath the trees.

Not even hand-in-hand. A proper distance between. And chaperoned. Not like so many young people today.

"Here we are, sir. Don't we have a nice library?"

Small, but carefully kept. Not many at the tables, reading—probably the celebration has taken the attention of most.

Over to the card file.

Marble, Markham, Marlborough, Marx, Groucho. Marx, Groucho. Marx, Groucho. Marx, Groucho. Mary. Mary.

The little woman at the check-out desk looks up.

"Are the cards on Karl Marx being retyped or collated?"

"No, we have no books on Karl Marx." She smiled pleasantly.

"Communism, then?"

"None on Communism either."

"Where's the chapel building, please?"

"I'll take you." It was the young lady again. "Vespers have begun. It will be filled because it's a special day."

Into the Gothic building, a stone in a green setting.

"God is love, love is God. God loves us, we love God. He understands us, we understand Him. He cares for us, we care for Him."

See God run. Run, God, run. Run, Run, Run.

"Peaceful peace from the God of Love. And now a closing hymn."

Follow the gleam, gleamel the foll, low the gleamoffel,

gloff the fleamow.

"Everyone is so quiet and reverent."

"Thank you, sir. We're quite proud of our chapel."

"Tell me, does he ever deal with problems?"

"Problems? What sort of problems, sir?"

"War, for instance."

"But he did, sir. Just now. You heard him mention peace, didn't you? He's always positive. Isn't that the best way? But perhaps there's some other problem you had in mind?"

"Race?"

"Oh, sir, you're funny. Of course we'll have a race. That's part of the celebration—the May-Day celebration each year. But there's no problem about race!"

"No problem, indeed. A race is a lot of fun. Now what do we do?"

"We hurry over to the maypole. There, do you hear the music? They've started already. Let's run. This is the big event of our May-Day celebration. We all—that is, the girls—get a chance to dance around the pole. See, there it is—over there, behind the dining hall. Isn't it beautiful?"

"Beautiful it is. And the music—it's lovely and quiet."

"That's our string quartet, sir."

"Do you have a rock group? Or folk music?"

"No, they're not permitted. But actually, even though some of us liked rock and folk music at home, we really prefer strings here. Sometimes we have a brass ensemble too. It stirs you."

"Aren't you going to join the dance around the maypole?"

"I'd like to. Will you excuse me for a few minutes, sir?"

"Of course. But come back."

Mayday. Mayday.

May Day, May Day.

Maypole, maypole. Over and under and up and through, near and beyond, far and down, past and by, forth and over and around and back.

"Back so soon?"

"Yes, I got tired. And besides, if we're not going to have to wait a long time, we'd better go over to the dining hall and get in line. You will eat with us, won't you?"

"If they're set up for guests. I really wasn't planning to stay for supper when I came, though."

"Tonight, guests are welcome. It's all part of the May-Day celebration."

"It's a pretty big dining hall."

"Yes, a thousand people can eat here at one time. But what takes time is going through the cafeteria line. Not that I'm complaining. They are really doing the very best they can."

The dining hall isn't open yet, but the line is already a block long. Yet it is quiet—orderly. No pushing or rowdy-ism.

"Everybody is so polite. And quiet."

"Of course. They discourage loud talking. And we want to do what they want us to do."

"After supper, what's on the program?"

"Something very special, sir. We have a drama group— I'm in it—and tonight we're putting on a play."

"Modern? Ibsen? Shaw? Miller?"

"No. Who are they, sir? Our plays are written by our very own Mr. Jackson. We also do Gilbert and Sullivan sometimes. But I can't sing, so I'm not in them."

"Do you ever have any protest meetings?"

"Protest? Against what?"

"This long line, for instance. Or the quality of the food. Or bigger things—national policy, things like that."

"Oh, no, sir. We would never think of protesting any-thing. We know they wouldn't like it. There, now, it didn't take us long to get inside the dining hall, did it? You can pay for your meal down there at the far end of the line, down past the steam table. Sometimes I work on the steam table. I sort of like doing that."

"Are you working your way through?"

"Working my way . . . ? Oh, there's someone I want you to meet. My counselor. Here he is. I don't know your name, sir."

"How do you do. I'm Muriel's counselor."

"And I'm just an out-of-town stranger, passing by. I saw the May-Day celebration sign, and decided to come in. And I'm glad I did. I'm really impressed. I have a daughter who is just eighteen—do you think she would be accepted here?"

"Is she somewhere else? I mean, would it involve a transfer?"

"No, she would be entering here for the first time."

"Well, the place to begin is to see your family doctor about commitment."

On the Train to Aswan Dam

MY HUSBAND and I had come as far as Egypt on our world tour.

Cairo was a whirling kaleidoscope of minarets and bazaars, camel rides, pyramids and Sphinx, with all the other tourist attractions that look so beautiful in the travel agency brochures but are so hot or windy or dirty when you experience them.

Finally we left Cairo for the Aswan Dam. We went south by train, and I must confess that I was relieved at the prospect of our long ride. I settled down on the seat with postcards and knitting and paperbacks.

I think Philip was restive—the track is rather straight, and the scenery monotonous. But for me, our compartment was a haven, the click-clack of the wheels against rails was soothing music.

At a dismal spot about a hundred miles south of Cairo, a place in the desert where we couldn't see the Nile, our train stopped. We didn't think anything about it at first—perhaps the train was taking on water, or running ahead of schedule. But after we had been there for an hour, and the air conditioning had stopped functioning, we realized that something was wrong.

The conductor spoke English, as if he were British instead of American—of course he was Egyptian. When we asked what was wrong, he was evasive. He apologized for the delay, said the engineer hoped to have the train moving again soon, but gave us no explanation.

Three hours later he stopped briefly to explain that the engine had some sort of mechanical difficulty. But it would soon be repaired, he assured us.

After five hours in that heat—it was over a hundred degrees—we were exhausted. Napping was out of the question, postcards were written, and knitting was the last thing I wanted to do.

Philip suggested that we take a walk, and so we went out of our compartment and stepped down from the train.

The khamsin wind from the south blasted us as if an oven door had been opened in our faces. We shielded our eyes with our hands against the sand and dust. Tracks stretched out ahead, tracks behind, the sandy desert as far as our eyes could see.

There was no activity at the engine—the engineer wasn't even around—so after we had walked a hundred yards toward the west, we turned around and came back to the train, kicking up sand as we walked.

The conductor was pacing back and forth alongside the coaches. We asked him where we could get some water to drink; by this time we were quite thirsty. He regretted that what little water had been aboard the train had been consumed. He was apologetic; he assured us that everything possible was being done to expedite repair of the engine, and said they hoped to make up time lost as soon as the train was moving again.

Once we knew there was no water, our thirst became much greater. Sitting in the compartment, we discussed what it must be like to die of thirst.

We also talked about the Children of Israel, wandering for forty years in a wilderness something like the desert that surrounded us.

"I wish Moses were here to strike a rock," Philip said—not irreverently.

By now it was late afternoon.

We tried reading aloud, but our minds weren't on the words we were saying. We discussed the Muslim religion, as we had so shallowly been exposed to it in Cairo. The hopelessness, the legalism, had impressed us. How different was our hope in Christ, we said.

But mostly we just sat silently, wishing we had a pitcher of ice water. Talking seemed to dry our mouths and make us more thirsty.

For a fleeting moment we glimpsed some Bedouins through the window; after looking at the silent train, they disappeared from view.

"Mind if I come in?" A young man, still in his thirties, spoke from the passageway. He was obviously American, his tie pulled down and his shirt open at the neck.

"Please do," I said.

"Of course," Philip added. "Especially if you have any information about when we can expect to be on the move again."

"I'm afraid I can't be any help along that line," said the young man as he came into our compartment. "I'm as much in the dark as you or anybody else. All I know is that it's a mechanical problem—not a change of government, or some Israelis blowing up the track." He laughed pleasantly.

Across the desert, the sun was getting lower. Inside the train it was now too dark to read. But the air was no less stifling, and when someone occasionally opened the door, sand and dust blew through the compartment.

"Are you folks headed for Aswan Dam?"

"Yes. Actually, we're on a world tour, taking it pretty leisurely. I sold my business a couple of months ago, and we promised ourselves this trip before I get into something else. I've still got ten years at least before I think about retirement. What do you do?"

"I'm a reporter for *The New York Times*. For the past six months I've been covering this part of the Arab world. It's not the best assignment, nor the worst. By the way, have you had anything to drink? If you haven't, you must be pretty thirsty by now. Let's see. . . ." He looked at his watch. "We've been stranded here for almost seven hours."

"No, we haven't had anything to drink. And in this heat, we've gotten mighty thirsty."

"Look, I came prepared. Back in my compartment I have four or five bottles from which you can take your choice. Come on back with me and we'll soon take care of that thirst."

I didn't say anything. I thought Philip should answer. After a moment's silence, he did.

"No, thanks. I guess we're not that thirsty yet. Unless you happen to have some ginger ale or other kind of soda."

"Sorry, I didn't bring any mixes. But if you object to strong drink, I have one bottle of dry Sauterne. You're welcome to it." There wasn't a shade of contempt or superiority in his voice—only a sincere desire to help us because he knew how thirsty we were.

"I guess we'll take a rain check on that." Philip said it easily, with a laugh. "But after you've been refreshed, why don't you come back here to talk. There won't be much else to do once it gets really dark."

The young man thanked us for wanting him to return, and left. We could hear him whistling a tune as he went down the corridor. We felt the blast of air and sand when

70

he opened the door to enter the next coach.

Philip and I talked about him for a while, wondered what his job was like, and discussed how we would approach him about spiritual things when he returned. It never occurred to us that he wouldn't.

It got completely dark, and we sat there unable to sleep because of our thirst and the heat. Several hours later I wondered if the young man was sleeping, his thirst satisfied.

Fifteen more hours passed before the train slowly started to move. That was after nine o'clock the next morning.

In all that time, he didn't come through our coach again. If he had, I would have seen him.

Rehoboam's Gold Shields

REHOBOAM checked in today, about four o'clock this afternoon. He walked into the dorm, looked around the way every freshman does, and headed for the room he'd been assigned to. Then he went back out to the car and brought in his gear.

Nothing unusual about Rehoboam's arrival—except that among his things were some gold shields. And those shields are the cause of no little comment around the dorm. He can tell.

A shield is an awkward thing, difficult to wrap, impossible to stow away so it doesn't show. Maybe Rehoboam wouldn't have been so conspicuous, if anybody else had brought shields. But nobody had.

"Why does a guy bring shields to a university?" he hears as he enters the john. But that's the end of the conversation, at least until he leaves.

Those first few days everyone finds some excuse to

come to Rehoboam's room. "What's the text for Chem 101?"

"When's the deadline for dropping a course?"

"Do you know how much an extra season ticket costs?"

Sometimes they don't even wait for the answer before they wander over to the dresser, where the gold shields are stacked. (The things are too wide to fit in a closet.)

"Hey, look at the shields," they say. "First ones I've seen here at the university."

Always there's the same feeble, half-apologetic explanation by Rehoboam. They were his dad's shields, but his dad gave them to him. Then he warms to his subject a bit and explains that they're really gold—believe it or not. Sure, they're worth a lot.

So they begin to call him the "Gold Shield Boy." Word gets out about the shields. Pretty soon it's all over campus—even the profs know. Worst of all, the girls think it's a big joke.

Hardly a day passes that one or two guys don't come over to Rehoboam's dorm to see the shields. Several upperclassmen advise him to hang on to them—"They're worth more than most of the garbage you'll pick up around here"—but the general opinion seems to be that shields are out of place in a university, and a man must be some kind of nut to own them. Especially gold ones.

After four or five weeks of this, day after day, night after night, a certain change begins to take place in Rehoboam. Defending his shields is wearing him down. He spends as little time as possible at the dorm, hangs around the union a lot and studies at the library. A conviction grows in his mind that he's a fool to have brought those gold shields along to the university.

One morning, as he dresses hurriedly so he can grab breakfast before an eight o'clock, he notices something. One shield is missing. Sure enough—it's gone. No time to look for it now, though. Later on, after class, he'll come back and find it. But later in the day, when he gets time to hunt for the missing shield, he can't locate it. And it doesn't turn up later in the week.

Before long, a second shield disappears, then another. Rehoboam is determined to keep the last one from being stolen, for he values that one especially. But when he returns to his room one morning at four a.m., after spending a night in town, he finds that the last shield is gone, too.

Surprisingly, his feeling, in the face of this great loss, is one of relief. Those gold shields won't make him stand out any more. Now he's the same as everyone else. At last he can feel thoroughly at home in the university.

And he does. The gold shields gone, his defense of them ended, Rehoboam becomes a popular figure on campus.

As Christmas vacation approaches, however, some misgivings trouble him. What to do about the shields when he goes home? His family will expect him to bring them back for the holidays.

The solution, when he finally thinks it through, is simple. He decides to replace the gold shields with others made of highly burnished brass.

He takes the counterfeit shields home with him when vacation begins, and his deception appears to be complete. None of his family seems to notice the substitution. This reaction pleases Rehoboam, for it would upset his family to learn of his loss, which he knows is a great one.

The Present

WHAT A BEAUTIFUL package. Look, each side of the box is different.

This side is white, pure white. I've never seen a lovelier young woman than the one sketched on the white paper. So innocent, so fragile, yet strong—with a trace of sadness about her face. Her features are Jewish, I think.

Turn the box around. There, that side is deep blue, midnight blue. Shepherds and their sheep. What a peaceful scene.

I wonder why this side is so dark. Nothing but darkness. Put it on the bottom so it doesn't show. Rest the package on that side.

That's better. Isn't this side striking? I don't think I've ever seen a more gorgeous shade of purple. It's—well—regal, especially with those men on camels in the design. I wonder where they came from, where they're going.

This gets more interesting all the time.

Look at this pure gold side. Those are angels, aren't they? This is by far the richest side of the whole package.

But what a contrast. This red. You know, I never did like red, especially that shade. I wonder why whoever wrapped this package, whoever designed it, made one side that awful color. Turn it away, turn the box so that terrible red is on the bottom and the dark side is at the back. There, that's much better; now the red doesn't show and the black side's turned away from view.

White, blue, gold, purple. I just enjoy sitting here looking at the beautiful package.

Aren't you going to open it?

Why—is there something inside?

Ceiling Zero

MY ROOMMATE is a guy named Gooley. Herb Gooley.

He transferred to this crummy little school in the boondocks about six months ago. When he first arrived, we were all asking why he left a big, well-known college at the beginning of his senior year. Everybody's heard of it; nobody's heard of us.

Only thing we have that they don't have is a flight school. What they have and we don't have would fill a book.

One night I ask Herb straight out, "Why did you come here?"

"One reason," he says. "Last Christmas vacation I learned to fly. So I decided to switch to a flight school, a place where everyone could fly. That's why I'm here."

I should explain that I don't mean flying planes, or gliders, or balloons, or anything. I mean we can fly, period.

We can step out of a window and be airborne. I remember my first flight—it was while I was still in high school—off a barn in the Blue Ridge Mountains. Some of the guys and girls here have been flying ever since they were little kids.

So the reason Herb Gooley gave for coming here made sense. Except for one thing, which he couldn't have known before he came. It's the sort of thing you don't learn from a catalog.

Gooley is a sensitive guy—withdrawn. Doesn't talk to many people. But there's some reason for being as he is: for one thing, he got off to a bad start.

I've never seen a happier freshman than Gooley, when he first showed up. I don't mean that he was actually a freshman—like I said, he was a transfer senior. But he had that same stupid innocence.

One of those hot afternoons in September—like so many days when school has just begun—I was stripped to the waist, arranging my clothes on hangers, when this new student comes through the window. He flew in—our room is on the third floor of Derwin Hall.

"I'm Herb Gooley," he says. "Boy, have I ever been looking forward to coming here."

"To this crummy school? Why?" I ask.

He looks sort of surprised. "Why, because it's a flight school. You can fly, can't you? The other guys in this dorm can fly, can't they? And the girls—just think of having a flying date. Wow!"

Should I tell him straight off, or should I let him find out for himself?

I guess I'm sort of chicken, because I decide not to say anything. Let someone else tell him.

"Yeah, this is a flight school, all right. We can all fly, including the profs—and the administration. You can have that bed over there by the door, Gooley. And that dresser, and either closet, except that I've got my things in this one.

The public relations department can fly, too. They prepare the catalog."

He doesn't say anything, but begins to unpack. First thing out of his suitcase is a copy of Aerodynamic Theory. It goes on his desk.

Around five-thirty I head for the dining hall. "Coming along?" I ask.

"Not yet," Gooley says. "Don't wait for me. I want to finish here first. I'll be along before it closes."

So I walk on over and go through the cafeteria line. I find my crowd and sit down to eat with them.

We're on dessert, when there's a little stir over by the door.

"What do we have here?" someone asks.

"An exhibitionist."

"A new student, you can tell that. Nobody else would fly on campus."

Sure enough—it's Herb Gooley, my new roommate. He comes through the door and touches down gently, by the stack of trays and the silver holder. He's got a smooth technique.

Everybody gets sort of quiet. I don't know about the others, but suddenly I'm thinking about some of my flights in high-school days.

"You're too late," this battle-ax who runs the cafeteria says. "We close at six-thirty."

The clock on the wall says six-thirty. She's absolutely right, which is what she always is.

"Serves him right," a girl going back for seconds on iced tea says, loud enough for Herb to hear. "He's just a show-off."

Gooley looks sort of hurt, but he doesn't say anything, either to battle-ax or to battle-ax, j.g. He just heads out the door. Walking.

"He'll learn," someone at my table says. "We all learned."

79

And he did, during the next few weeks.

First thing he finds out is that here nobody flies. In spite of this being a flight school, and everyone can fly—theoretically—we're all grounded.

There's a lot of talk about flight, of course. Flight courses, references to flight in a lot of other courses, a daily flight hour. But nobody flies.

Some of us came here planning to be flight instructors. I myself wanted to teach Africans how to fly, but that didn't last long.

Actually, the deadest things are the flight courses. They use Aerodynamic Theory as the text, but you'd never recognize it. One flight out of a hayloft has more excitement to it than a year of that course.

One night we get into a discussion on our floor of the dorm.

"Look, Gooley," one of the guys says, "tell us about the college you were in before you came here. Is it true that they have more exciting courses than we do here?"

"A lot of them, yes," Gooley says. "But they don't know anything about how to fly."

"Are the girls there real swingers?"

"I guess so. But they can't fly."

The way Herb answers sort of frustrates the guys who are asking the questions, because they would jump at a chance to transfer to the school he came from.

"I think this flying isn't all it's cracked up to be," one of them says.

"I feel the same way," another chimes in. "And besides, it seems sort of selfish to me to fly when the rest of the world is walking."

"Not only selfish—to them you look like some kind of a nut, up there above the ground. From here on in, any flights I take are going to be when there's nobody around to see me."

"Besides, the world needs to be taught how to walk.

80

And pavements and roads need to be improved."

"Did any of you read John Robin's book? It's a pretty strong critique of Aerodynamic Theory, and he does an effective job of questioning the usual foundations of flight. The significant thing is that Robin is a flyer, not a walker."

That was the only time I ever heard Herb Gooley swear. "Oh, hell," he says and dives out the window. (It was a cold night, but fortunately we had opened the window because the room was getting stuffy. If we hadn't I think Herb would have gone right through the glass.)

He didn't return until early next morning. I heard him at the window and got up to open it. It had begun to snow, and he was covered. He looked nearly exhausted, but happier than I'd seen him since the day he first arrived.

That night marked a change in Herb Gooley, a change that came to affect the whole school. Only, I didn't know it at the time.

He began to fly again. On campus.

Now when you're with flyers, flying isn't remarkable—actually it's the basic minimum, it's taken for granted. What worries us is perfection, and it's sort of embarrassing —around other flyers—to try an extra little maneuver, or to stay aloft longer than usual. There can be such a letdown. And the competition is so keen. There's always someone who can fly better than you.

That's the reason nobody flies here. At least they didn't, not until Gooley took it up again.

Like the flight prof says, "This is a school for flying, not an airport. You've come here to learn more about flying, not to fly. We want to teach you how to fly with real conviction." Then he draws diagrams on the blackboard. And he walks across the campus.

Meanwhile, Herb is getting better and better. I mean his flying is improving. You can see him on a moonlit night, trying all sorts of flight gymnastics.

Moonlit nights. That brings me to another side of the change in Gooley.

He began to have flying dates. Not many—none of the girls, except one or two, would be caught dead on a flight date, especially with Herb.

What can you talk about on a flying date? What can you do? I ask you.

We discuss it while Gooley's out of the dorm. He's out a lot those last months of school. Not just flying or on flight dates, but teaching a bunch of kids to fly at the community center in town, studying Aerodynamic Theory with a little group of students. The guys can't understand why Herb keeps at it.

"Sure we can fly—at least as well as that guy Gooley. But after all, real life is down here on the earth. It's not as if we were birds."

"Besides, we've got to learn to relate to the walkers. And that's a lot harder to do than flying."

"I've found—I don't know about the rest of you guys—but I've found that they're not much interested in my flying ability. I mean, the walkers aren't. So it's important to show them that I can walk."

"Don't get me wrong, it's not that I'm against flying. I'm not. But you don't have to fly to be for flying."

So the year ends.

We graduate.

I ask Gooley, while we're packing, what he plans to do next year.

"Grad school," he says. "In a walking university. You see, I was reading Aerodynamic Theory the other day, where it says that you can take off best against the wind."

Birth

WRETCHED PLACE to be delivered. Birthplace of oxen, of asses, of vermin. Pain. Travail in a stable.

Fear not, Mary.

Stench of manure. Straw, pungent, acrid. Birth pangs in a stable.

For thou hast found favor with God.

Pain. My first baby. A boy. Born in a stable, born away from home. Nine months. Nine long months.

Thou shalt conceive in thy womb, and bring forth a son.

A son. My son. Strange thought—not his. Pain. My son, my Savior. Our Savior.

Thou shalt call his name Jesus.

Jesus. Jesus. Pain. He shall lead our people into the Promised Land. Beautiful name. Jesus, my first baby. A boy.

He shall be great, and shall be called the Son of the Highest.

God's Son in a stable? Birthplace of oxen, birthplace of vermin? Pain, what pain. Son of the Highest.

The Lord God shall give unto him the throne of his father David.

Palaces, not stables, for kings. Pain. Pain. Stables for asses, for sheep. For a little lamb.

Of His Kingdom there shall be no end.

David's kingdom ended. Every kingdom ends. Pain. His Kingdom . . . Pain. It will never end. Never. Pain. Greater than King David. Pain. Pain. My baby. My Savior. Pain. Pain. Pain. Joseph, *Joseph.*

My baby. Those fingers, so tiny. Round little arms and legs. My baby.

That holy thing that is born of thee. . .

Cover him up. Wind it tight. Drafty old stable. Stars through the roof. Smelly manger, hard and cold.

He shall be called the Son of God.

Those hands, those tiny, perfect little hands. They made the stars, the earth. God's Son, my Savior, my baby. It's cold tonight. Cover the hands, too.

Protest Until Pizza

"So WHAT ARE you going to do?"

"Do? What can I do—what can anyone do? It's done now, over, finished, kaput."

"No marches?"

"Are you kidding?"

"No placards? No demonstrations?"

"Look, about that seventeenth-century lit assignment. . ."

"You're a great one. March for better food in the dining hall, march for Prof. Fliedner, march for graffiti on the library walls. Now suddenly, halt, one-two."

"Come off it. Let up, will you? Those things were free speech. This would be free suicide. Anything now would be putting our heads in a noose. Besides, I didn't see you at any demonstrations, even the big sit-in for Fliedner. You never carried a placard for free speech. So don't start trying to make me feel guilty. By the way, what do you intend to do now?"

"Nothing. I'm not going to change my pattern, which means I'm consistent."

"So am I. It's just that a new element, a radically different element, has entered the picture."

"Meaning Irving was dragged out of the dormitory?"

"Right. That and the Supreme Court decision last Friday. Now there's no longer any doubt about it."

"But what happens to free speech, if that's so?"

"It's still there. Nothing's happened to it."

"Provided you use it harmlessly—like trying to get visiting privileges in the girls' dorms extended to all night or something else that's strictly university."

"Sure, like that."

"But not Irving, picked up by the federal police last night. Not the prison camp outside of Peoria. Not the genetic tests of fallout."

"Cool it. After all, I can't do anything about those things."

"You mean they're not like getting more steak in the dining hall, or pressuring the university to renew Fliedner's contract after they discover he's a Communist?"

"Right. There's some hope for results on protests like that. But Irving, prison camps—no hope. Absolutely none."

"What if Irving's headed for the extermination chamber?"

"All the more. Who knows—say I did protest—that the federal police wouldn't be knocking on my door tomorrow night. Then my days of usefulness would be over."

"Just like Irving's."

"Sure, like Irving's. Only he had no choice. I do."

"Thank God you're not Jewish."

"Right. And you can, too."

"I do. Never more than today. But I got sidetracked. We were talking about demonstrations and free speech."

86

"You were talking. I'm finished."

"Don't you feel any responsibility to demonstrate against the government's policy toward Jews?"

"What good would it do?"

"I don't know. I guess it wouldn't change things."

"Right. And the Supreme Court's decision makes it pretty final."

"So Irving is thrown to the dogs."

"He has lots of company, if you've been reading the papers."

"But I know Irving personally. He's someone I've gotten my physics assignments from. I've talked about the World Series with him. I've eaten pizza late at night with Irving."

"But he's Jewish, and there's nothing you can do about it."

"I'd like to make a sign, 'Free Irving Greenhow,' or 'The United States is Murdering Jews,' or maybe even, 'Get Haman out of the White House.' "

"What would you do with the sign?"

"Why, I'd carry it downtown—maybe to the newspaper office. Then I'd march with it."

"For two minutes maybe. After that you'd be on your way to Peoria. With only your teeth smashed in, if you were lucky."

"But what a glorious two minutes! It would almost be worth it."

"Nothing's worth dying for."

"But Irving's not a thing. He's a person endowed with certain inalienable rights."

"Not any longer, he isn't. He's a nonperson without any rights at all. Maybe he's dead already."

"So steak is more important to you than Irving."

"I guess so. Or—give me the benefit of the doubt—Fliedner's right to teach although he was a Communist? Some of the protests were more significant than others."

87

"You'd demonstrate for Fliedner's right to speak, but not for Irving's right to live?"

"I wouldn't put it quite that way, but I guess that's about it. The point is, we had a chance of gaining what we were after in Fliedner's case; none at all in Irving's. So why demonstrate?"

"Maybe to let them know we don't agree with what they're doing to the Jews. Or to say—here's Irving Greenhow—he's got as much right to live as anyone else. As me. Even as the President."

"But he doesn't. The Supreme Court answered that question last week. The Bill of Rights is relative; it's conditional."

"Isn't there any higher appeal than the Supreme Court?"

"Not in this country, there isn't. The Supreme Court is the end of the line."

"I know that. But beyond the court, even beyond the country. Isn't there any higher authority?"

"The UN stopped meeting two years ago. What's left?"

"What about you and me?"

"What about us?"

"Don't we have any responsibility to a higher authority?"

"Who? If you mean Irving—if you mean human dignity or something like that—it's too late. He's probably dead. Or soon will be."

"I mean God."

"God? What's He got to do with this? God's in church on Sunday mornings, not in demonstrations. God isn't carrying any placards. Not even for Irving."

"Maybe I owe it to God."

"Owe it to God? If you did, the preachers would be telling you, don't forget that. They're not."

"Maybe they value their lives as much as we do ours."

"Of course they do. If they got killed, or even put in

88

prison, who'd keep church?"

"So everybody is silent because they—I mean we—might get killed if they spoke."

"Not might. Would. There's no doubt about it."

"That means life is more important than anything else in the world."

"Right. You'd better believe it."

"It also seems to say that life is more important than God."

"And it is, except for some misguided people in history who had a martyr complex."

"Including Jesus?"

"I don't really know. He's a hard one to figure out."

"He didn't keep silent."

"And died for it."

"You know what? We've been talking so much we missed supper."

"Let's go downtown and get a pizza."

How Shall We Remember John?

MY BIG BROTHER JOHN and I were great pals. In fact, our whole family was close, including Mom and Dad, my sister, the brother I'm telling you about, and me. We were close in a way that you find few families today.

Breakfast was always a special time. We sat around this round oak table with a red-checked cloth on it. Mom almost always served the same thing: steaming hot oatmeal with brown sugar cooked in it (we piled a lot more on top of it, too), and milk. A big white pitcher full of milk.

We'd talk about what we were going to do that day, and maybe we'd joke some. Not that we had a lot of time—we didn't, but we had enough to talk some before Dad went off to work and us kids went school.

John and I were two grades apart in school. That was sort of hard on me, because the teachers who had had him were always comparing us when I got into their class. And the comparison wasn't too flattering to me.

Don't get me wrong. John wasn't a teacher's pet or bookworm. He was a regular guy, and the kids all liked him, including the girls. Maybe one guy who was sort of a bully didn't, but everyone else did.

Life went on like that—breakfast of oatmeal and milk, walk to school, classes, walk home, chores, supper, study around the kitchen table—and you never thought about anything else. Except vacation. Vacation was always stuck in your mind.

You know the kind of life, day after day, when it's so great you hope it never ends. Maybe you cry at night sometimes if you ever think of your Mom or Dad dying—you know they will someday. But then you go to sleep, next to John, who's already sawing wood.

It was Christmas vacation, when I was in sixth grade and John was in eighth, that it all suddenly came to an end. Actually, it was two days after Christmas.

John and I had gone to ice skate on Big Pond. It was a real cold day, cold enough so that your scarf got ice on it from your breath. I put on my skates in a hurry and sailed out to the middle of the pond. I noticed a slight cracking sound from the ice, but it wasn't much and I wasn't worried. It had been pretty cold for about a week. So I showed off some for John, who was still lacing up his skates, sitting on a log, and then I headed for the opposite shore.

John stood up and went real fast, right out to the middle, too. Just as he got there, I heard this sickening cracking noise, the ice broke up, and John fell through.

I got a long branch and went out as far as I could on the ice. But I couldn't see John anywhere. He had just disappeared. I yelled for him, and I went even farther out, but he wasn't there.

I must have panicked, because first thing I knew I was running into the house shouting for Mom, crying my eyes out, yelling that John was in the pond. It was awful.

They found his body later that afternoon.

A few days after the funeral, we were sitting at the table, eating breakfast one morning. Nobody was saying anything, all of us were thinking about that empty chair over against the wall.

You could tell Mom was trying to talk. Finally she just sort of blurted out, "Look, we all miss John, terribly. We loved— love him, and we'll always miss him. Now I have a suggestion to make. Do you remember how he liked oatmeal and milk?"

"Do I!" I said. "I sure do. He used to pile on the brown sugar until—"

"That's enough. He liked his oatmeal sweet and so do you. What I want to suggest is this. Let's think about John every time we eat breakfast. Let's remember him whenever we eat oatmeal and drink milk. Let's talk about him—"

"Yeh, like the time he and I went swimming in Big Pond and. . ." I knew before Sis spoke that I had said something I shouldn't have. Everyone was sort of choked up.

"Time for school," she said.

And Dad said, as we all left the table, "We can continue this later."

Well, we did. And we agreed with Mom's suggestion. So each morning, when that big pitcher of cold milk went on the table, and our bowls of steaming oatmeal were set in front of us, we'd talk about John.

It wasn't sad talk, but happy. Remembering. I don't mean we never said anything that made us choke up—other people beside me did. But mainly it was happy talk. And we still talked about what we were going to do that day, and even—after awhile—joked some.

One day, some months later, Mom said, "You know, I don't think what we're doing is quite respectful enough for John's memory."

"Respectful?" I said. "Why, it's fun. Sometimes it's almost like John is here with us. I like it."

"So do I," Mom said. "But I think we're too casual about it. So I think we ought to set aside a time when we're not rushed like we are at breakfast. Let's say Saturday morning. And we'll remember John in a more fitting place than the kitchen. We'll sit in the parlor, and we'll have a special time worthy of John's memory."

"Aw, Mom," I said, "John always liked breakfast in the kitchen. Lots of oatmeal with plenty of brown sugar on it. And milk. Why make a big deal out of it?"

"That's enough, Son," Dad said. "We'll do as your Mother says."

So every Saturday morning, after we had eaten our regular breakfast in the kitchen, we went into the parlor and remembered John. Mom had gotten some little silver cups for the milk, and some tiny plates for the oatmeal.

Later we only went into the parlor once a month, instead of every week, and now we only do it every three months. It doesn't seem right to me, but I'll soon be leaving home, so it doesn't much matter.

I still wish we had never begun that "fitting" remembrance, and had just kept on remembering John every time we ate breakfast.

Still Small Roar

IN THE KINGDOM of ideas lived a word.

The word was unspoken in real-world language, not through mere ignorance, but through inability to contain it.

Thus the word continued in the unapproachable realm of ideas.

Now other words were easily contained, readily expressed. These were the dread words, the dead ones, fearsome, morbid, evil, beautiful.

There were a few in the real world who affirmed the unspoken word's existence. "It is there," they said, "even though we cannot perceive it. We are in a box that excludes the word. We cannot break through to it, but it is there. Just outside the box."

Some vaguely felt their need for such a word, although they had little hope that the word really existed.

But the other real-world inhabitants, in overwhelming

numbers, denied that there was such a thing as an unspoken word. "Whether the word is or not makes little difference," they said. "What counts is here and now. Go back to sleep, or to sex, to stocks or clubs, even to rosebushes. Why waste your mound of minutes with a word that isn't spoken? There are enough other words to satisfy—three- and four-letter words, seven letters, even twelve-letter ones. And for all and always, the single-letter one."

Those who knew the four-letter words, and the twelve-letter ones, were least interested in the unspoken word.

And so it continued from generation to generation. Words became longer, new words were formed, the one-letter word continued at the center and perimeter of life in the real world.

Still the word continued unspoken, and hope dimmed among some who had affirmed that there was such a word.

Others, the feeling and sensitive ones, shaped substitute words to which they gave allegiance. "It has come out of the idea world to reality," they said. "The unspoken word has finally been spoken"—but it hadn't. And no new word survived prolonged encounter.

One day the word was spoken.

In a whisper.

This surprised everyone, but most of all those who had insisted that there was such a word: they expected a shout, a roar, a waterfall thundering of sound.

And the whisper was first heard in a barn.

In a real barn, in a whisper. When the word left the barn, it went throughout the countryside. Country people heard it, not kings—the small, not great.

"Yes, it's the word," they said, "the word we never knew we wanted because we never knew it was."

They took the word from a barn into their peasant homes. It was spoken at their tables, their picnics, their weddings and funerals.

Strangely, the four-letter-word people heard the word most eagerly. The fifteen-letter people scorned it, explaining it away.

More strangely, most of those who had lived expectant for the unspoken word now refused the spoken one. "This is scarcely the word we awaited," they said. "It isn't even shouted."

And when the word was shouted, they said, "It shouts against us. The word has no sense of the appropriate, the significant." Thus they showed their disappointment with the word.

"If it were really the once unspoken word, it would conform to our expectations. Since it doesn't, it can't be. We prefer no word to this word we hear."

Those who had most wanted the word to be uttered came to despise the uttered word. They scorned it and turned from it.

But to those who listened, the word was powerful, more powerful than howling storm or waterfall, marching army or creeping lust.

And the power was implosive; the word shattered all other words. All of them, but especially the one-letter word. That one was formed anew around the now-expressed word, concealing the word that it revealed.

What was true of the one-letter word was true of the rest. Even the four-letter ones were changed, made beautiful, by the spoken word.

Those who turned from the word were irritated, then aghast that such a thing should happen. "Four-letter words are to be buried, not changed. The one-letter word is to be affirmed, not torn to shreds."

"And besides," said others, "if it were the true word, it would be spoken in temple and palace, not hovel and sailboat."

Children loved the word. They laughed it, sang it, danced it. And they could understand it, even when the fifteen-letter-word older people were puzzled at the word's meaning.

"It means 'I love you,'" they'd say. "It means 'Come here. Don't be scared.'"

For the people were afraid.

"What will the end be?" they asked. "The word casts doubt on all our other words. It is not at home in the real world, yet soon it will fill our every nook and cranny."

At increasing pace, resistance to the word—bitter, vengeful, calculated resistance—grew among the people.

"The word could destroy us," they said. "We have no choice—come, destroy the word. Our world is at stake—or be destroyed."

And so, impelled by hateful fear, or fearful hate, temple and throne joined to destroy the word.

And they did.

They erased it from pavement, wall and book, that word first whispered in a barn. They silenced it, whisper and shout, from hill, field, lake, desert, tree.

They erased the word, expunging hope. For while the word existed outside the box, within was hope, dim hope. And when the word was spoken, hope flowed.

But the word removed killed hope.

Children and four-letter people cried for the word that no longer was, the hope that was dead. So did some five-and seven-letter ones.

The twelve-letter and fifteen-letter people decided that they should bury it. For it was a worthy word, they agreed.

They put the word in a dictionary, contained it with all the other words. That seemed to be the proper place for it, a place that was safe. "After all, a word is only a word," they said. "And all words are on an equal footing in a dictionary. So that's where the word belongs."

But the dictionary couldn't contain the word, nor could all the dictionaries. It broke out, grew, and filled the box.

The word broke out of the box and left a gash through which the beyond idea world could be glimpsed for the first time from the real world.

Children waited wide-eyed, looking up at the gash. In all their games and hurts they watched the gash.

"We'll hear the word again," they said. "Next time it'll roar. And it will tear up the box."

Black Gold

JUDSON DORMER came out of China in 1949. He was swept out by the Communist regime, along with thousands of other missionaries and their dependents. They left the church behind, its hospitals and schools and other institutions possessed by the enemies of God.

After a short rest in the small town in upper New York from which he had first gone to China, and to which he had returned several times on furlough, Dormer began to accept meetings in various places. In the early fifties, people were immensely concerned about Communism, both in China and also in our own country. Senator Joseph McCarthy was then alerting Americans to the danger of our own Trojan Horse.

So this returned missionary, Judson Dormer, was much in demand as a speaker. Primarily he took church engagements, but he also spoke at Kiwanis and Rotary and other service clubs, as well as at high school assemblies.

Let me tell you, he was an imposing person. He had what we've come to call charisma, at least as far as I understand it. He stood up there on the platform and looked you straight in the eye, and you just had to believe that what he said about the Red Menace was true. When you went home afterward, like I told my wife, even the headlights of passing cars looked red.

I guess the big reason for this was that Dormer had himself suffered at the hands of the Communists. He was able to tell us what they were like up close.

First time I heard him was at Second Church in Iowa City. I had supported his missionary society for some years—actually, it was one of the first obligations we had taken on after we were married—and so I decided to drive in to the meeting when I heard he was to be there.

Marian was in the midst of canning, and she said, "You go alone. I can hear him some other time." So I got into the pickup truck and drove into the city by myself.

A lot of speakers start out by telling how glad they are to be in Iowa City, or feeling at home in a Baptist or Presbyterian Church. Or they tell a funny story.

Not Judson Dormer. He stood up there in the pulpit, right after the pastor had introduced him, and looked us straight in the eye. He was silent for maybe a minute, then he held up five slender, pointed sticks.

"These bamboo rods," he said, passing them from one hand to the other, "were pounded down under my nails with a hammer by my Communist jailers. They interrogated me for as long as fifteen hours at a stretch, trying to get me to deny my faith and admit that I was an American imperialist agent. But God brought me through, and I'm here tonight to warn you that what happened in China can happen tomorrow—tonight even—in the United States of America."

He told us how he had been arrested at the missionary

compound, separated from his wife, and hauled off to prison in an army truck. He was in that prison for ten months, he said, and those months were the closest thing to hell that anyone could imagine. Interrogations for long periods of time, under a single light bulb, with teams of fanatical, sadistic Communists taking turns questioning him. Almost daily beatings, living in an isolation cell with only a bucket: these were the things he endured.

Those bamboo sticks pounded under the nails were almost the least of his sufferings. He could not describe others in a mixed group. (He probably could today, things have changed that much.)

I don't remember everything he said that night, but I do remember thinking, during my fifty-mile drive back home, that America was in tremendous danger. I also thought how proud I was, although that may not be the right word, to have had a part all these years in his mission's work. I might be an Iowa farmer, but I had done something to stem the Red Tide in China.

When I pulled into the yard, I went right into the house, not even stopping to check the barn. I headed straight for the kitchen.

"Marian," I said, "did you ever miss something tonight. Judson Dormer was just great. You'll have to go tomorrow night."

"I will, if I get this canning done," she said.

She was tying spices up in a piece of old sheet to put in the vinegar that was boiling on the stove. It smelled good, like fall.

"Look," I said, "you've got to go, whether it's done or not. I almost feel ashamed of myself, coming back to the land and cattle and house—even cucumber relish—after what I heard tonight."

"Tomato relish, green tomato relish," she corrected me. "What did this man have to say?"

So I told her, as best I could. By the time I finished,

101

she was ready to call it a night and go to bed.

The next night we both drove in to Iowa City. If anything, he was better than the night before, including more details of his ten-month imprisonment.

We went up to the front to speak to him after the service was over. I introduced myself and Marian to him, and told him how much his messages had meant to me. He looked me straight in the eye and said, "Don't thank me, thank God."

Then he asked me what I did, and I told him about the farm. I didn't say much, because there were other people waiting to shake his hand. I also told him that we had supported the work of his mission in China for a number of years.

Before he turned away from us, Dormer took out a little black book and asked me to write down our name and address. The book was filled with other people's names.

Driving home, I asked Marian what she thought about Judson Dormer.

"He is certainly a good speaker," she said. "He holds your attention, and you're surprised, when he stops, at how long he's spoken. At the same time . . ."

"What?" I asked. "Was there something about him you didn't like?"

"Not really." And I couldn't get anything more out of her.

To Marian's credit, in all the years since, she hasn't once mentioned the misgiving, or early warning signal, she had that first night. But that's the sort of woman she is.

A couple of months later, we had a letter from Dormer. It wasn't on his mission's letterhead—in this letter he told how the Lord had led him to establish a new work, an independent testimony to the faith. He called it "Truth Against Communism," and there was also the verse on the letterhead, "Ye shall know the truth, and the truth shall make you free."

He appealed for money to support his work, and of course we added him to our list of missionaries and Christian works. This wasn't too hard, since the corn harvest that year was especially good and prices were high.

I'll pass over the next few years, only explaining that every fall Dormer returned to Iowa City. The meetings outgrew Second Church, and were held in the Municipal Auditorium. Thousands of people heard him and hundreds became members of Truth Against Communism. (For a ten-dollar contribution, you got a membership card for your wallet, and a subscription to *Alarm!*—his monthly paper.)

One fall when he was there, he accepted our invitation to come out to the house for dinner. It was a long trip out and back, but he seemed to appreciate getting to see the farm, and—of course—Marian's cooking. We had a steer butchered and put in the locker that week. So we had some good steaks. And, recalling that first night I ever heard Dormer, I got Marian to break out some of her green tomato relish.

After dinner, while Marian was getting ready to go in with us, I took Dormer for a little walk through the pasture.

"You know," he said, "I grew up on a farm. It wasn't at all as big as this; farms in New York State usually aren't. It's a very simple life, but once you leave it, you never can go back. Shanghai, or even Iowa City, I guess, gets in your blood, and you're sunk."

I must admit, when he said that, I felt a little dissatisfaction with my life. What had I done, where had I been, except live in Cambridge, Iowa, all my life? Still, when I thought about it later, I got some satisfaction out of thinking that Marian and I had at least sent our money to China and the Congo and other places, to serve the Lord there.

One day, about four or five years after we had first met Dormer, we had a different kind of letter from him. The letterhead said, "Reclamation Mining, Ltd." Judson Dormer's name was there as president, and the address was a Canadian one. I had a moment of surprise that he was in business rather than his anti-Communism mission work, but that was soon dispelled. I kept the letter—here it is.

Dear Brother and Sister in Christ:

As you know, I have given my life to stamping out the brushfires of Communism in China and the United States.

One serious obstacle to mounting an all-out attack on the enemy is the lack of money. This is true not merely of Truth Against Communism; it is true of every other work of the Lord.

How much more could you do if you had ten times as much money—even a hundred times as much money —to give to the Lord's work as you are now giving?

God has now made that possible. I am writing to let you know about a miracle by which your money can be multipled like the Loaves and Fishes.

As you doubtless know, there are many worked-over gold mines in the West. They are worked-over, but not exhausted. Hundreds of millions of dollars worth of gold still lies there, some on the surface, some underground in abandoned mines, just waiting to be reclaimed.

Why was this gold missed? Because it was too expensive to separate the ore. And it would still be too expensive if it were not for the miracle I mentioned.

That miracle is a new mining machine, representing a totally new concept in ore separation, that has just been invented. I am teamed up with the inventor (his name is at the top of this letter, as vice president and treasurer) and we are announcing the availability of shares in Reclamation Mining Ltd., on the following basis.

1. Anyone may invest at $1,000 a share (Canadian or American). You may buy as many shares as you wish, with the following proviso: Since I want this whole project to benefit the Lord's work, every investor must agree to give a minimum of ten percent (a tithe) of the profits to Christian work. You need not give this to Truth Against Communism, although I hope many of you will do so.

2. For every $1,000 you invest, I guarantee you will receive $500 *per month,* starting one year after you have bought into the operation.

3. Anytime after six months, you may get your money back, with ten percent interest per annum, simply by requesting it.

Some of you may want more information about the Miracle Machine. I regret that I cannot describe it for you, except in the broadest terms. The inventor has no intention of even registering it for patent purposes, since that would enable any unscrupulous person to duplicate it.

But I can tell you that a prototype is now operational. I have seen black ore transformed—by God's wonder of modern technology—into the purest gold. Gold, I might add, that is like the product of suffering in the Refiner's fire.

We will soon be closing this offer, so I appeal to you not to be overly long in deciding to invest . . . for His kingdom and your financial independence . . . .

I read that, and I read it again. Then I took it in the house and got Marian to read it.

"What do you think?" I asked. "Do you think we should invest?"

She folded the letter and put it back in the envelope. "You've decided about buying the farm and farm machinery and cattle up to now. You're the one who decides when to sell the corn. And I've been pretty well satisfied. So I don't see why I should have to be a part of this decision. You make up your mind and I'll go along with it."

"But we'd have to mortgage the property."

"If you decide to mortgage, I'll sign for it with you. But you decide."

Two days later I went to Cambridge State Bank and arranged for a $7,000 mortgage loan. I explained that it was for investment. Since we had finished paying off the old mortgage on the property several years before, I had no trouble getting the money.

I had the check made out to Reclamation Mining Ltd., and sent it off air mail. I enclosed a short letter to Judson Dormer, explaining that Marian and I were with him in this, and that we wanted seven shares.

A few weeks later, we got a receipt for the money.

The next year passed pretty fast. That was the year we had torrential spring rains, and you couldn't get a tractor into the fields until late in May. Whenever I got worried about the crops, I'd think about our shares and be at peace. That's how much confidence I had in Judson Dormer.

As the end of the year approached, Marian got enthused, too. We'd talk about what we'd do with the money after we paid off the mortgage. One thing was to buy a camping trailer. Another was to increase our giving substantially—way beyond the tithe—to the Christian works we were interested in.

I never expected a check right on the anniversary of our investment. But when two weeks passed, and then a month, and then two months, I began to get a little concerned. So I wrote a letter to Judson Dormer, asking if maybe the check had gotten lost in the mails.

Several weeks later I had this mimeographed letter from Dormer in reply.

Dear Friend,

Unexpected complications in securing machine parts have delayed our reclamation mining project.

I regret that this has delayed the payments on your investment that I guaranteed. This is doubtless a disappointment to you, as it is to me.

Be assured that we are working night and day to become operational, and will keep you informed by regular progress reports.

It will be worth it, I think you'll agree, when your monthly checks begin to arrive . . . .

I hated to show the letter to Marian, but I did. She just said, "I guess all of life has its complications. So we shouldn't be surprised if this does, too."

Six months later, we had another mimeographed letter. This one was signed by Ernest Madling, Certified Mining Engineer.

Dear Investor in Reclamation Mining Ltd.,

At the request of our mutual friend, Judson Dormer, I am writing to give you my professional opinion about the ore separation process and related machinery in which you have purchased shares.

The process is absolutely sound in chemical engineering theory.

Of more importance, I have seen the machine working at an abandoned mine in the West. (Discretion forbids my identifying its location more precisely.) Quality and quantity of gold reclaimed from the ore are excellent . . . .

Well, that encouraged us. So we just waited eight months more, and had the mortgage on the farm converted to run a longer term. It still wasn't easy making the payments.

By this time, I was writing to Reclamation Mining Ltd. every six weeks or so, sending a letter to Truth Against Communism at the same time. The last letter I sent, I asked them to return our total investment of $7,000, as Judson Dormer had promised he would at the very beginning. I sent the same letter to both addresses, by registered mail.

When this letter produced no results, I wrote to the missionary society Dormer had served under in China. They replied that he had resigned from the mission about six years earlier, and they regretted that they could supply no information about him.

A month or so later, reading the Saturday Church News page of the Iowa City paper, I noticed that a missionary of this society was going to be speaking at a church there the following day. So Marian and I drove in to that service on Sunday morning, instead of our own church in Cambridge.

The missionary was good, but I could hardly wait for the service to end. I wanted to ask him a lot of questions.

Marian and I waited around until everyone else had left the church, except a few people talking at the front. Then we introduced ourselves to the missionary.

"I'd like to ask you about one of your former missionaries," I said. "That is, a former member of your mission."

"Judson Dormer?" he asked.

"Yes. Do you know about his mining project?"

"That's why I thought you wanted to ask about him. Did you invest any money?"

"Seven thousand dollars. Is there any hope, do you think, of getting any of it back?"

"I'm afraid not. I was just up in Canada, and it's a pretty big mess. If an investor who's Canadian would lodge an official complaint, the government would investigate. But nobody will."

"How about here in the States?"

"It was a Canadian operation. The Securities and Exchange Commission won't get involved. Incidentally, I lost two thousand dollars myself. Money I had saved for retirement."

"I'm sorry. With the farm and all, it isn't so serious for us."

Marian had been silent up to this point. But now she said, "You know, it's sort of strange how he hoodwinked us—and a lot of other people, too."

"No doubt about it," the missionary said. "And most of the people couldn't afford it any more than we could."

"Makes you wonder," Marian continued, "about all those other things he told us—about the things that happened to him when the Communists took over in China."

The missionary was quiet for a few moments. Then he spoke. "You know, he never was in any Communist prison."

"He wasn't?" we both exploded.

"No, he made that whole story up. Very few people in the mission even knew that, and when he resigned, our leaders decided not to say anything about it. I guess they thought he was no longer answerable to them, and it would be an act of Christian love to cover it up."

"Love for whom?" Marian asked. "The people who believed him and supported Truth Against Communism, and later invested in his mining scheme?"

"Nobody could have known at that time—before it all happened—how it would turn out," the missionary said.

"What about that report from the certified mining engineer?" I asked. "He said the machine really worked."

"Ernest Madling isn't a mining or any other kind of engineer," the missionary said. "He's a pastor out in the prairies. Dormer evidently persuaded him to write that letter and sign it as he did."

"Do you have anywhere to go for dinner?" I asked.

"We're going to eat here in Iowa City before we head for home, and we'd like to have you join us."

"Sorry, I'd really like to," the missionary said. "But I'm going home with the pastor."

So we said goodbye and went out and got into the pickup truck.

"Do you know what," Marian said, "you're going to take me to the best restaurant in town for Sunday dinner."

"Sure," I said. "Anything else?"

"Yes, one more thing. I liked that missionary. He wasn't flashy, but he had a lot to say that was worth saying. I'd like us to think about giving to his support."

The dinner was great, except the relish wasn't as good as Marian's.

Afterword

JESUS taught in parables.

Why?

The most obvious reason is that everyone likes a story. Child or grownup, sophisticated or uncomplicated, formally educated or wise in the experiences of life: Interest mounts, the guard goes down when someone begins to tell a story.

Campfires predated auditorium and lecture hall by millennia; the storyteller came before preacher or teacher. Stories are entwined with the roots of culture, of religion, of civilization.

And we remember stories.

They turn up expected or unannounced in the mind's recall. "That makes me think of a story" recurs in conversation and in life.

Jesus told the kind of stories people don't forget—about two sons, a house without foundation, an absentee

111

landlord, a vengeful servant, a man who got involved when he needn't have. Across the years and changes of life, Jesus' stories touch the nerve of human existence; they are transcultural and transtemporal. (Abraham Lincoln's stories are probably remembered for the same reason.)

But this is only part of the truth. From His total teaching, we know that Jesus didn't need to tell stories to hold His listeners' attention. He had it regardless of literary form. Nor were His stories unique in their power to compel remembrance. Hungering for righteousness; bread, wine, whited sepulchers; God's watchfulness over the sparrow, His beauty in the field lily: the illustrations and imagery Jesus used program the mind for associational recall no less than His stories. So do His historical and topical allusions.

A parable is more than a story.

It is a story on target, set to shatter any listener who gets in its way. Yet a parable's trajectory is unpredictable, except to One who knows a man's secrets.

Like God knew David.

David, friend of God, military tactician, powerful ruler, adulterer, instigator of murder.

How would you bring such a man to reality and contrition for his sins? I don't know what you or I would have done—probably we'd have preached a sermon at him, or quoted some Commandments.

But God sent a prophet, Nathan, to tell David a story. The story was actually a parable aimed at David's heart.

"There was this man," Nathan said, "who had so many sheep and cattle that he couldn't count them. And there was this other man, a poor man, who had nothing except for one little lamb.

"That lamb meant everything to the poor man and his children; it was the family pet. The man used his savings to buy it, and his children sacrificed some of their food to keep it alive.

"One day a visitor came to the rich man's house. The rich man wanted to give his guest a good meal, but at the same time he hated to deplete his flocks or herds by killing a single animal to do it.

"So he went to the poor man and—because he had the power that usually accompanies wealth—he took the little lamb from the bosom of that poor man's family and killed it. He killed the lamb and dressed it and served it at his own table."

King David's anger erupted.

"As God is my witness," he said, "that rich man shall die, and four lambs from his flock shall be given to that poor man's family. What kind of a man is he, who has no pity on the poor, no compassion for a family that has nothing except one lamb?"

"Thou art the man."

With those words, Nathan's parable exploded in David's own breast. It was too late for him to get out of the line of fire.

Here is a parable's uniqueness: It is about the only way of obtaining objective assent to truth from one who is personally involved. Judgment is passed before the judge realizes that he is the accused.

Jesus got behind masks with His parables. He got through to the individual in the crowd. Everyone enjoyed the story; one or two got the explosive point. They were the ones tuned in, the ones with "ears to hear," wills to obey.

Another value of the parable is that it can say something different to a variety of listeners. It can home in on more than one target. For example, Jesus' parable of the prodigal son is not quite the same story to a rebellious boy, a worried father, and a self-righteous, self-pitying older brother. It is subtly different to a person without any family relationship. To a variety of listeners, the parable says, "Thou art the man."

Or to none. The clever person, the one who knows all the angles (especially in his dealings with God) can step out of any line of fire. He can miss the point (God lets him), which does not prove that the point is not for him, but proves rather that he refuses to become involved with an idea he has already rejected.

Parables may veil as well as reveal the truth. Jesus explained that He told parables to those who were not chosen to know the mysteries of God's Kingdom, "that seeing they might not see, and hearing they might not understand."

A parable tags the right person, but does not let the rest go free; it ties them with stronger bonds. Parables seem to elicit a deeper response to truth than mere intellectual assent.

A parable has one other great advantage for religious communication. It is open-ended. It avoids the trap of a lot of our writing and preaching. (A college student described most of the sermons he hears as "First, second, third, and home.")

Andre Gide says that great writing involves a flash of insight by the reader, discovery of something he thinks the writer didn't realize he was saying. Such writing opens a door, not into a closet but into the wide world, the timeless, placeless world. And beyond.

Closet-writing (or preaching, or thinking) ties things up in a neat little package: "This is it, this is all there is of it. Here's your answer and why should you want to think or imagine anything beyond? 'This do, and thou shalt live.'"

The package goes into our pocket or purse, safely contained outside ourselves. No fear of its exploding in our breast.

Marshall McLuhan suggests that in today's communications climate the neat, tight package may be suited to hot media, such as radio or a recording. But it is a failure in cool media: speaking directly to an audience, television, or even writing. When reader or listener has to fill in details, McLuhan says, there is greater interest and freedom.

The passive reader wants packages; the one who is interested in pursuing the subject, or in seeking something beyond, wants the open-ended, the incomplete, the germ of an idea, the sort of situation that requires participation in depth.

Here is the power of parable.

For me, the discovery of parable has been akin to my awakening one summer morning twenty years ago, in a small room of a pension located in the village of Gruyon, Switzerland. I threw back the covers, left my comfortable bed, opened the curtained window—and clouds came floating past my eyes, just outside my little room on the mountain. Through the clouds, a thousand feet below, I saw a green valley, chalets, cattle grazing. Beyond the clouds, I saw the eternal Alps.

My simple act of moving from a warm bed to the window, opening it up and looking out gave me all this.

Are all the stories in this book parables?

You tell me the answer to that question now that you've read them. Or let me examine your pockets, your chest.

Maybe there isn't even one parable in the lot.

JOSEPH BAYLY
Bartlett, Illinois

THE PICTURE BIBLE

FOR ALL AGES

If you've just finished this book, we think you'll like its companion in the

CHURCH/FAMILY-IN-ACTION SERIES

CAMPFIRE COOKING. Looking for ways to make good-tasting, practical meals a part of your camping ministry? Do you know what utensils, what cooking facilities you'll need, how a family or church group can get the most out of its money and time? Good recipes? The answers are all in this book!
75937—Paperback; 128 pages. $1.95

CAMP DEVOTIONS. The beauties and wonders of nature appear in Jesus' teachings, an appeal that reaches young people especially well today. This guide for the outdoor worshipper helps you pick an appropriate spot, find a devotional text and lesson to match it . . . so you both teach and learn!
75945—Paperback; 128 pages. $1.95

(Ready April, 1974)

You can order these books from your local bookstore, or from the David C. Cook Publishing Co., Elgin, IL 60120 (in Canada: Weston, Ont. M9L 1T4).

---------------------- **Use This Coupon** ----------------------

Name _____

Address _____

City _____ State _____ Zip Code _____

TITLE	STOCK NO.	PRICE	QTY.	ITEM TOTAL
Campfire Cooking	75937	$1.95		$
Camp Devotions	75945	1.95		

NOTE: On orders placed with David C. Cook Publishing Co., add handling charge of 25¢ for first dollar, plus 5¢ for each additional dollar.

Sub-total $ _____

Handling _____

TOTAL $ _____

If you've just finished this book, we think you'll agree . . .

A COOK PAPERBACK IS

REWARDING READING

Try some more!

HOW SILENTLY, HOW SILENTLY by Joseph Bayly. Fantastic entertainment . . . with meaning YOU decide! Thirteen tales of mystery, drama, humor, science fiction lead to discovery.
73304—$1.25

FAITH AT THE TOP by Wesley Pippert. From a seasoned Washington reporter . . . a look at 10 eminently successful people who dared to bring Christ with them all the way.
75796—$1.50

LOOK AT ME, PLEASE LOOK AT ME by Clark, Dahl and Gonzenbach. Accepting the retarded—with love—as told in the moving struggle of two women who learned how.
72595—$1.25

THE 13TH AMERICAN by Pastor Paul. Every 13th American is an alcoholic, and it could be anyone. A sensitive treatment of alcoholism by a minister who fought his way back.
72629—$1.50

THE EVIDENCE THAT CONVICTED AIDA SKRIPNIKOVA edited by Bourdeaux and Howard-Johnston. Religious persecution in Russia! The story of a young woman's courage.
72652—$1.25

LET'S SUCCEED WITH OUR TEENAGERS by Jay Kesler. Substitutes hope for parental despair—offers new understanding that exposes the roots of parent-child differences.
72660—$1.25

THE PROPHET OF WHEAT STREET by James English. Meet William Borders, a Southern Black educated at Northwestern University, who returned to lead the black church in Atlanta.
72678—$1.25

WHAT A WAY TO GO! by Bob Laurent. Your faith BEYOND church walls. Laurent says, "Christianity is not a religion, it's a relationship." Freedom, new life replace dull routine!
72728—$1.25

THE VIEW FROM A HEARSE (new enlarged edition) by Joseph Bayly. Examines suicide. Death can't be ignored—what is the Christian response? Hope is as real as death.
73270—$1.25